Got

a novel by

D

The Armory
Brooklyn

Published by Akashic Books
©2007 D

ISBN-13: 978-1-933354-16-3
ISBN-10: 1-933354-16-X
Library of Congress Control Number: 2006901899

First printing

The Armory
c/o Akashic Books
PO Box 1456
New York, NY 10009
info@akashicbooks.com
www.akashicbooks.com

Start

You've got this thing about Thursdays. One day before the weekend. One day before you get paid. You get past Thursday and the week is really over. But if something fucked-up happens then it almost always ruins the stretch that follows it. So when it comes to that day of the week you try to be extra careful.

You take your time getting out of bed. You stretch before you do push-ups. You have a bowl of cereal before you leave the house. It's the one thing you're a little obsessive about. Everything else you're willing to let ride.

Funny thing is that your Thursdays belong to someone else, someone who controls almost everything in a certain world, a world where you live for a good part of the time, a man you never ever planned to cross, until the two of you collided in the middle of someone else's game, a game that ended with the end of the world as you knew it.

Thursday, September 11, 2000

You've been doing the job longer than you want to think about. The bags are always waiting when you get there. Sometimes they're leather, sometimes the cheapest nylon. But they always weigh the same. Always exactly the same.

You've come a long way from the days of smash-and-grabs down at Union Square. You refined yourself beyond boosting whips at the Meadowlands and pushin' smoke to the trust fund babies at NYU. Any more of that and you were never going to see twenty-one. So there was only one answer when the question got popped like a bottle. It's only ninety minutes out of your day and they pay you a grand a week, in Benjamins. How the fuck could you ever beat that? Plus the job has a special perk.

She's about five-six with legs that taste like chocolate, eight-pack abs, and an ass that even she admits is hard to carry. Her green eyes glow in the gelled light overhead and her lips . . . well . . . her lips are the best part of all.

First time you met her was by accident. She was coming out of the spot when you were on your way in. Jeans and a sweater underneath that Dior trench, wine-colored pumps with fur on the heels. Her hair was a dark brown with cranberry extensions weaved into her cornrows. And she had a book in her hand. *One Hundred Years of Solitude* in its original Spanish. If that didn't call for bonus points then what did? Half black, half Dominican She told you to come see her sometime. So you came, a lot.

She was a good reason to do some budgeting. You cooled down that fetish for sneakers and jeans, so she could make your snake stretch. You put the phone, cable, and Internet together in one bill so you could come home with that scent that only dancers wear, that flower-bomb knockoff shit that comes in the translucent yellow bottle. You bought her some for her birthday, or at least on the day she told you she was born.

The best thing is that you don't have any illusions about the arrangement. You're paying for it and you know it. You're paying to see her move. You're paying for the touch of her flesh against your palms, the feeling of her sweet breath on the crucial parts of your lower anatomy. You pay for the daylight delusion that she belongs to you.

You can't wait for her fingers to wrap around

your wrist as she leads you between those walls of tinted glass. You keep the bag closed, right next to you and in reach at all times. She pours you a Hen and Coke to go along with whatever playlist you've chosen for the hour: "Your Body's Callin'," or "How Do U Want It." Sometimes you take it old school with that "Voyage to Atlantis." You stay up half the night before trying to put together the perfect mix. You want each time to be perfect in a completely different way than the time before.

She doesn't actually dance for that long, just enough to get your pulse rolling, just enough for you to forget about what you've done since the last time. She crawls to you, her wrists and thighs gleaming with oil and glitter in the sparse light coming down from above. She takes her time lowering your zipper and then a deep breath before ignition. Her breath is so warm you imagine your dick fogging up like glass in the dead of winter.

Then she locks lips together, forming a union between her and your most prized possession, the bar through her tongue running up and down the elongating speed bump on the underside. You feel those press-on-nailed fingers working the balls underneath, squeezing them as she effortlessly travels your length. You hear yourself moan without recognizing the voice. You clench the extensions on the back of her neck like they're a horse's reins.

She removes the sequined fabric that separates her tits from your line of vision. They fall like fruit from a tree, hanging perfectly just above your palms, her plum-colored nipples hardening as you make contact. Titties swing in unison with her head and neck, rolling to the rhythm of the music she can't hear through your iPod. The Whispers are "In the Mood."

This started out a one-time thing all those weeks ago. You made your drop early and the club was close, so you decided to come through. At first you only watched her from the stage. You watched the way all those bitch niggas just stared like she was something they could never have. You put 20s in her garter every ten minutes, blowing your bonus before it even got warm. An hour later you'd have her up in the room, one-on-one in a five-by-eight box.

Every week she brings up a different outfit: garter belts and stockings, leather g-strings and the plastic stuff that chick wore in *The Matrix*. Her fingers and toes are tools of precision. Her rear teeth are in perfect alignment.

She tells you about all the niggas and broads that want to steal her away from this place so they can put her in their own cages. She tells you this because she knows you respect her, because you know that outside of here she's just another girl bound to give you broad-type problems.

It's your twelfth week here and you still don't know her name—her real name, that is. You don't know how long she's worked there or where she was born, how old she is or if she's got rugrats. All you know is that she's good, and for now that's all that matters.

You lean back as her saliva flows, as the slip and slide gets more intense. Your feet fall in opposite directions as you get that feeling, that faint rumbling in your nuts begins to build, rising to the top like Doug E. Fresh's third-most-famous single. One hand pinches her nipples. Another grips the ungrippable left cheek of her divine ass.

You imagine that you're inside of her, fuckin' her from behind, her face pressed against the tinted glass, that perfect cleft between her ass cheeks widening as she moves back and forth, pulling you into the depths with your hands as the steering wheel. It becomes more real than where you really are. She is goddess.

You come like you haven't fucked in a year, and she takes it all, what she can't hold spilling down the sides of her mouth. You black out for three seconds, and when you come to she's spitting it all into what looks like a plastic shopping bag. She must have stashed it under the chair.

"Good?" she asks, retying her sequined top. Her face's sprinkled with tiny beads of sweat.

"Good," you say, breathing heavily and blushing. You would give her anything, anything in the whole fuckin' world.

"You comin' back next week?" The words don't surprise because of what she says, but how she says them. There's a twinge of something questionable, something diversionary, something to keep you in your place just a little longer than usual. That intuitional reaction then becomes concern, which almost immediately makes itself over into full-blown warning.

Her eyes move away from yours as you consider what might have just happened. Then something catches your eye beyond the one-way glass. Two shadows are moving quickly, moving as if they're making a beeline for anywhere away from where they are. You reach to the right for the bag but it's not there. The entire week's drop for Brooklyn is not next to you, a drop that totals at least four times your annual salary.

You shove her against the glass and head out the doorway, not staying long enough to see where she lands. You button your pants without zipping as you move toward the spiral staircase. One foot drops in front of the other as fast as you can make them.

You go down the stairs (losing your iPod somewhere in the process) and past the first bar and then through the main lounge where all the working dudes are blowing their checks. One takes his hard dick out and shows it to a dancer. The bouncers are on him before he gets a single stroke off.

All the men in this room are too old and too slow, muthafuckas who might've done this a lifetime ago, but not now. They've got families and kids and mortgages. There's way too much to lose after forty, no matter who you are. Something tells you to get to the parking lot.

This is one time when you really wish you had heat. I mean, you're dealing with two dudes at least and there's no telling how well they're armed. But you stopped fuckin' with burners a long time ago, for reasons you'd rather not go into here and now. Triggers get awful light when you've got good aim. And when you've got good aim the list of targets can be endless. Too much blood. Too much gear set aflame to get rid of the evidence.

Two shadows turn the corner of the building

as you clear the push-bar exit. You pick up the pace, measuring out each stride as you sprint in their direction. When you turn the corner you almost slip on what appears to be a black wig made of cheap plastic hair. Are these dudes actually broads or is this meant to throw you off? Are you running after the right muthafuckas, or is your bag already in a car headed in the opposite direction?

This shit is like a bad dream if you've ever had one, one of those really mindfuckin' ones you get on the nights you don't go to sleep high. That's actually why you always try to go to sleep high—cuz then it's nothing but black space and the sound of your own snoring.

There are no streetlights in the alley but you can see their slender silhouettes heading toward the mouth at the other end. You put on the Jedi hyper-speed. Maybe you can catch up to them, tackle the one with the money, and watch the other bitch run off glad he/she's still alive.

The thought of something that perfectly easy makes you grin as you run. The grin narrows your eyes in the relative darkness and you fail to see the seven-foot dude with the double barrel stooped down less than ten feet in front of you. But you do hear those barrels roar when both shells explode, forcing a countless number of tiny ball bearings into you at the speed Superman is said to have beat.

Less than a moment later you, like the man of steel, are flying, backwards toward the bulbs above the parking lot, that blinding fluorescent glare just below the stars. The Brooklyn night is so clear, so beautiful. Maybe it's the last one you'll ever see. But not likely. You're wearing Kevlar. No guns, but you never go without a vest.

Somewhere in the distance a car turns over. They, whoever they are, are getting away. You can also hear the sirens in the opposite direction. They'll have questions and you better make up the perfect answers. Because sooner or later Star will start wondering where the drop is. And you know he ain't gonna take no excuses. He might, however, take your life.

So you'll have to run until you catch them, whoever they might be and wherever they might go. There could be others, all of them armed to the teeth. Your ribs could be cracked or even broken from the blast. But that don't even matter in the scheme of things. You've got about ten hours until dawn, ten hours to get that bag and get it to the man who lets you live and pays you as a favor. So you best better start moving.

1.

There are about six cops in front of you, their pieces and shields blocking you from those you have to chase after. Some of the faces look familiar. There's Mike, the lil' skinny Colombian kid that couldn't hoop if his life depended on it, and Andre from Armstrong Houses. Andre was the first nigga you ever fought, the first nose you made bleed on that second grade strip of asphalt during recess. The other faces are familiar enough, all from the hoods where you grew up or close by, all from families left broken by what Brooklyn used to be for the young, hungry, and colored, before it became "The New Manhattan."

"So why were you wearing a vest anyway?" Mike asks, taking notes on his little soldier pad. You tell him that you're a black man living on one of the darker parts of Pacific Street. You say that your cousin died a year before in Chicago, that the two of you were like brothers, that once he went you thought your number might be up. You explain that you're just a student and show them your ID, going on and on about that degree in Marine Biology you're working on at a school that doesn't even offer the subject as a major. But they don't know that. So fuck 'em.

One of the guys you don't know says that witnesses saw you running through the club. You explain that your boy called you on the cell and pretended as a joke that your car was being towed. They ask if you think he could've had something to do with the shooting. You tell him that he's a family man, that he only did it because he was mad that you were at the strip club while he was at the crib dealing with the wife and kids.

They ask for a name. You give them one and a number that matches it. The person who answers will cover for you, because he owes you. Shit, when you think about it, a lot of people owe you. Tonight might be the time to call in some of those favors.

The pig's questions continue. At least one of them has seen you associating with associates of the known felon you work for. The others at the very least know that shotguns ain't a part of a small-time robbery where they don't even take anything. They ask you if you know what the shooter looked like.

"Yeah," you say, "he was a dude in a dark alley

with a shotgun." One of them laughs. He's the one that's probably scrambling to find something to bring you in on.

"Hey, we're trying to help you," Mike says, taking a step forward so he's the closest one to you. "You should tell us everything you remember."

You want to say that you remember when he used to push weed out of his cousin's hooptie in front of that rib joint on Gates. But instead you keep it real businesslike.

"It happened so fast, dog," you begin. "I'm goin' down the alley to my car and somebody hits me up with a twelve-gauge."

The medic who's been taping you up this whole time turns to the gang in blue and announces that two of your ribs are indeed cracked. The pain is a bitch and you won't be able to fill the prescription for a proper painkiller until morning since you won't be going to any hospital—not right now, you tell the medic. He gives you a shot but says it'll wear off in a few hours. Thus, pain will be a part of everything ahead. Everything.

"You're not giving us a lot to work with," Mike says, speaking for the half-precinct all around you. "But we'll follow up and let you know if we find anything out."

"I appreciate that, officer," you say kind of sarcastically. Even Mike knows that it's silly for you to not call him by his first name. But your association is from a long time ago. From y'all being boys. And now you're young men, men on opposite sides of a thing that neither person can describe.

The others back away one by one, heading to their cop cars. But before Mike does the same, he kind of leans in toward you. You can smell the nasty aftershave he wears as he slips you a tiny piece of paper.

"Let me know if you need shit," he whispers. "For real."

You put the paper in your pocket, knowing you'll never dial it. The cop you know can be far worse than the one you don't. He shakes your hand to give him the cover of being a good protect-and-server and then heads back to his vehicle.

They all pull off, fading into the night like the moon into a sunrise. You ain't had to talk to cops in a long long time, not since that shit in Harlem all those years ago.

"It's gonna hurt," the medic says to you as you start to stand up. He gives you a box of gauze and some tape and says that you're gonna have to come to the hospital in a few days to get your ribs looked at again. You tell him you will, though you probably won't, and then he's shutting the rear doors behind you and climbing into the passenger seat of the ambulance so his partner can return them to what remains of the night.

Everything shuts down as EMS leaves the scene. The neon sign announcing the club goes out like a blown candle. Maybe the owner has been told by your employer to wrap it up early. Maybe Star already knows about what's gone down. The entrance lights go out next. Then it seems like every parked car comes alive and pulls away, all while you're standing there trying to figure out your next move. You become a shadow in a part of town populated by other shadows.

You head down the block to where you parked your jeep, the '78 Range Rover everybody clowns you for.

"That shit ain't classic," your boy Rich said once, before he got killed. "That shit is just a clunker."

You would've come up with a better line had it been you, but then again he was a bitch-ass nigga from Trenton. Who the fuck tries to rob a convenience store with a knife? And besides, style is for suckers. They may laugh at your shit, but they don't know about that enhanced V-12 you got under the hood. That makes it faster than anything they've got. Plus it's solid steel so it can take a hit. Two features that just might come in handy if you're ever being chased.

You turn onto Woodbine to see your baby right where you left her. The tinted windows are still intact. No dents. No scratches. No smashed mirrors from anybody who got too close. She is ready and waiting for the night ahead. All you have to do is climb inside.

Once you get in, Fate will bring you back to the money before the powers-that-be come a-knockin' on your windshield. You reach into your pocket for your keys, losing yourself in the one moment when you might see them coming, the two creeping up behind you and the other one crouching on your passenger side. But that moment comes and goes and the first one barely misses you with the club aimed at your head.

It isn't so much that you sidestep the blow as it is that you move opposite of the direction he expected you to. But when that wood hits asphalt, you know the drill. You step on the club before he can raise it again and he loses balance, ending up on his ass.

The other hits you across the face with a hook that stuns, but your block absorbs the worst of the impact. Then you kick him in the balls.

Club Boy tries to get to his feet but you shut him down with a kick to the face. Your only mistake is reaching down for his club. It gives the enemy time to rally themselves. It also gives the dude hiding behind your truck time to get you with the stun gun. After that you descend into darkness.

You come awake in a room you know all too well, the one that smells like tuna and roach spray. You've seen the glass-framed posters of Jayne Kennedy, Lola Falana, and Sheryl Lee Ralph every week for two years, images capturing memories of beauty long gone. Falana got Ms. Kennedy started looking like Mo'Nique. And Sheryl Lee Ralph got on *Moesha*.

You know the rusty-ass stapler on the desk hasn't been used for binding paper in years, but it played a hand in somebody's death just after Easter. This is Tony Star's office. This is the den of the lion whose loot you just lost.

He comes into focus as you sit up in your chair. He's wearing a brown herringbone blazer and matching pants with an *Atlantic Star* T-shirt and a greasy texturized chili-bowl fade. He ain't no fashionista, but he doesn't have to be. He controls all the barrels that are most likely pointed at your head, and he's eating what appears to be a peanut butter and jelly on whole wheat and sipping from a drink box.

"My kid left her lunch here," he begins, talking with his mouth full. The colors you can see between tongue and teeth are disgusting. "Figured I might as well not waste it."

You think to yourself that he could use the meal, especially when he's five-eleven and around 155 soaking wet. Yet and still, he's been shot three times, stabbed once, and his first wife tried to poison him for fuckin' her sister. Knowing all of this, you know better than to speak first. That gets you a guaranteed knuckle sandwich. He'll drag this out, mix fear and tension into a cocktail ODB might have been afraid of. He chews and takes one big gulp of a swallow.

"You been makin' runs for me clean as a whistle two years straight now. Never short. Never late. No complaints. Right?"

You nod ever so slightly.

"Yeah, that's right," he says, as if to confirm your gesture. Then he pauses again to suck the drink box dry. According to the labeling it's passion fruit, a strange flavor for a kid to break out at the lunch table, or at least you think so.

"So I been tellin' myself that somethin' ain't right. That you just too clean for your own good. Now I see that I was right. Or am I?"

This is where you're supposed to start explaining.

You tell him that you got got, that you were coming out of the spot and got hit by some dudes for the bag.

Apparently he doesn't buy it. Before you can finish the last sentence somebody brings a metal folding chair down on your skull. The blow is so hard that two of the chair legs underneath you snap from the impact, spilling you onto the hard floor.

After that everything in the room is brushed with greens and purples. You're pretty certain that another one of those is coming, and sure enough it does, across your back and left shoulder. Your head rings like a bell and your eyes won't focus. The words *brain damage* keep going through your mind like a CD stuck on a scratch.

The final blow (or blows) will most likely be delivered by Mr. Star himself. Or at least that's how it always happens in the movies.

"You been the most honest muthafucka ever work for me. Why start lyin' now?" he says, the Caribbean coming out in his speech. "You think I ain't got eyes on you? You think I ain't know when that bitch ran off with my bag?"

You don't know which part of it to react to

first—that you've been tailed or that he let this broad get away with his money only to crucify you for it. But he doesn't want an answer just yet.

"Hey, if the bitch sucks your dick every week, that ain't got shit to do with me. I don't give a fuck about that. But when she gets ahold of my drop, running a heist with the fuckin' bartender? Now that's some other shit all fuckin' together. You shoulda had that bag cuffed to your wrist. But then again, for that kinda money they might've just chopped it off."

"I went after 'em," you murmur. "And I almost had her when some nigga hit me in the chest with a twelve-gauge."

"You shoulda got the fuck up and got my paper instead of waitin' for the fuckin' pigs to ask you all them bloodclod questions."

You realize that there's some sympathy somewhere, that if there wasn't you'd be dead already or on the way to some wooded stretch in LI or South Jersey where they'd strip you naked and leave you with nothing but a plastic tarp and a hole in your dome. But he just keeps talking. And there's something about it that says you're gonna live, for a little bit longer at least.

"You had till 2 to make your other stops. You shoulda got on the phone, called a nigga and . . ."

You miss the rest, as a construction boot

comes across your face. In a beat or two you can taste blood and a broken tooth.

"All you had to do was pick up the phone and dial the fuckin' number and shit wouldn't be like this," he repeats.

Something that feels like a lead pipe comes across the other side of your rib cage, the one that isn't cracked. You let out a sound that reminds you of a little brat's temper tantrum. Then a weighted fist slams down on your jaw with the force of an A train.

You think about that DVD you forgot to send back, that broad with the perfect tits you booked at Wood's party the weekend before and how she probably would've sucked your dick if her girls hadn't been hating. You think about the salmon ravioli at L'Express you couldn't eat now even if you had an appetite since your spit is probably redder than the marinara. You think of the way it felt when you came in her mouth just a few hours before, how it almost seemed worth all of this.

Then they stop. Your eyes are squeezed shut. Everything hurts. Everything trembles. Multiple footsteps move away from you. A door shuts. And there's nothing left but Tony Star's voice, the mixed scent of peanut butter and jelly, liquor, roach spray, and your own spit forcing its way into your nostrils. These are the last words you hear before you lose consciousness again:

"You got till dawn. Come back empty-handed and I beat you until your limbs fall off. Maybe I sell your organ to make up for what you made me lose. You got that long cuz I like you. Cuz I think you got a future. Prove me right."

You fall into the darkness again like a long-needed sleep. Somewhere in a dream you see the girl you're after, the way that ass shined beneath colored lights, the way you wanted those heels locked behind your neck while you fucked her until her disks ruptured. What a dream that was. If only you could live there forever.

2.

When you open your eyes you're in the driver's seat of your own truck, dried blood crusted around your mouth, grains of broken tooth between lip and gum. Both sides of your torso hurt too much to think about, and it feels like you've pulled your right hamstring. All of these injuries and you're supposed to track down thieves and get a bag of cake back that might already be halfway spent. Hand-to-hand combat is definitely out of the question.

You're about to break a rule you've had for years, since that night at Skate City, since you almost died. You never even wanted to see a gun again. But rules are made to be broken when your life is on the line. So there's somebody you're gonna need to see.

It even hurts for you to turn the key in the ignition. That little twist of the wrist actually makes you feel pain. Damn, they fucked you up good. Real good. And there ain't shit you can do about it but keep on moving. This whole thing makes you think of that dude with the African name, the one you went to see that one time. He took out that board and those shells, and for 120 bucks he told you what you already knew, that being in the streets wasn't for you, that you had a bigger destiny than bleeding to death on some corner over work that wasn't even yours.

He'd said that too much of that was already in your blood, that you had to be the one to change things, to get out of crime and into something respectable. Away from hustling, away from long cons and low blows in the middle of the night. And you were all for that, until tuition time came. You wanted to learn but the payments were killing you. You felt like your old man on wednesday nights when he did the bills. It sucked to always have to short somebody.

What is there to say about your daddy? That he was tall and real dark, that he had a lazy eye and bowlegs, that the only thing you remember him doing was fuckin' your mother right in front of you, not with the door open, not while you were asleep on the couch, but putting his dick in her whenever he felt like it, even if you were watching TV right next to them, even if he'd rented their bedroom to one of his boys and decided to use yours—while you were still sleeping in it. You were nine years old then. He smoked Newports and drank Crown and didn't seem to shower so much.

You found his body on your thirteenth birthday. You had snuck out of seventh period, crept across the playground, and came back to the crib to run a little Super Nintendo, and you found him laying there, right by the door. You remember the holes in his chest, so big you thought they'd come from a gun, but somebody had stabbed him—with a long blade, somebody said. Through the rib cage and up through his vital parts. You envied them, cuz you wouldn't have minded doing it yourself.

You found out at the funeral that he had a piece of some storefront church, that he and some other dude went in there and preached. They took up a "special" collection for the building fund that didn't build nothing but their bankrolls. The man could quote the Bible in his sleep but you never ever saw him pray. You never saw him or your mama talk to God.

Dear ol' Dad, the muthafucka you looked way too much like, the one who came to you in your dreams sometimes and told you that you thought you were better than him, that you couldn't get away from the blood in your veins, that you were gonna grow up to be just like him. You woke up with your heart racing, wondering if it was real, wondering if he was right.

Moms hadn't been too much better. But what the hell could you have expected from a teenage girl with dyslexia and an ass like an apple (or so people around the way told you). She was a lot of things but definitely not the type to call up one of those career training centers that advertise during the soaps. That shit was way too hard and time-consuming. And for the kind of shit she wanted it was downright impractical.

She's kinda foggy to you now, actually, even more a blur than your daddy was. But you remember the lips and the tits, the two things she never gave that you desperately needed. No loving kisses and she always fed you out of a can. Bedtime was at 1 a.m. on school nights and Popeyes was your favorite thing to have for breakfast. You remember the smell of the coffee grounds she used to pack the work in before taking it to the post office. Maybe that was before they put dogs to all the packages at the postal service. Or maybe she was lucky.

The one thing you respected about her is that she didn't fuck in your bed after he died. As a matter of fact, you never saw her with a man at all after Dad, even with those fuck-me pumps she used to have on with her titties hanging out, skirts so tight she could barely walk in them, and doll-hair extensions down to her ass.

There must have been some boyfriend in the mix, somebody who was keeping you in Trix and Lucky Charms, or maybe those were the names of the powers she had at her disposal. The only time you had together was when you'd take those bags to the aunt-of-the-week at Port Authority and roll up to Albany posing as whoever it was' kid.

The best trip was when you saw the black girl blowing the white guy in the seat across from you. You remember how thick and moist her lips seemed, how even at seven or eight you envied that man more than the kid in your class that had all the *Star Wars* toys with half the He-Man collection thrown in for good measure. It was so worth it the first time a chick blew you, that Haitian girl with the light eyes and legs that stretched on forever. But Mom and Dad were both dead by then.

At least you hadn't been there when Mom met her end. A shot in the arm made to look like an OD. But you would've remembered the tracks if she was a real user. You would've remembered that vacant look in her eyes or the nod that always goes with H. Nah, somebody wanted her out of the way. You were just glad you didn't have to ID the body, that you heard it from the social worker, the Italian one with the body that made her seem black. You still keep the letter in your glove box so you can read it once in a while and remember what little of her is left. For some reason you tell herself it was all his fault, even though somewhere deep down you know that they were what they were: a match made in Heaven.

Shit got even worse after that. Two years in three different group homes: the kid with the missing eye who jerked off under the stairs three times a day, the half-white, half–Puerto Rican dude with the Batman hairline that was always into sniffing rubber cement, the big thirty-year-old lookin' nigga that stole your Walkman and split your lip open, the one whose arm you broke with the metal bat in that softball game six months later.

Then it was *Diff'rent Strokes* time, time to move up to the better part of Bed-Stuy. Nice little couple. The teacher and the contractor. You always suspected that he was into getting tied up. You'd seen the rope marks on his wrists at breakfast, or the marks on his face where there might have been a gag. Big six-five 250 nigga into being treated like a bitch. Go fuckin' figure.

But that shit was way better than the group home or the people that birthed you. You had your own room and dinner every night. And there were books all over the place, ones with spines intact. Christmas and Thanksgiving dinners. A suit of your own for church a Sunday or two a month.

They showed you how to pray. They showed you how to study. You saw the degrees on the wall framed in glass in their little home office, and for some reason they meant something, something you wanted. Sometimes you didn't even like going to school cuz you were worried that you might leave and come back and they wouldn't want you anymore.

Your foster father once sat you down and explained why you were there, that he'd been like you, a ward of the state who had to fight for his life to get out of that world and into a new one. And he wanted to give someone else the same shot he'd gotten. Brothers didn't always look out for one another the way they should. And he refused to be a part of the problem.

You went to work with him in the summers, lifting hundred-pound wood posts and breaking up cement with a jackhammer. You knocked down walls and nailed in joints. You learned how to mix paint and a little about electrical wiring. You learned enough in one summer to be a laborer for life. He made you feel proud of yourself.

She was such a frail little thing, short and slim

with a smile bigger than anything else on her tiny frame. Something told you that she couldn't have kids, that deep inside she wished they'd adopted someone younger, someone she could raise instead of repair, something smaller to press to her bosom and pretend that she could feed it.

She could still cook her ass off though. Sometimes you'd just sit in the kitchen and watch her panfry fish and steam vegetables. You'd ask all of these questions like you were still eight, like you were trying to catch up on all the things the woman you came out of had failed to provide.

After those eight years you believed in salvation because you'd been saved. The hand of God had pulled you out of Hell and into a place that was only missing the feathered wings. You had a 3.2 average senior year and a full scholarship to Brooklyn College. You had proved your old man wrong. You hadn't turned out like him.

But right after freshman year, Hell came looking for you again, a few months after that night at Skate City. You were at some house party, easing your fingers into a girl named Terry, that Trini chick with the Hindu tattoos on her thighs, thinking that the road to penetration was almost to an end. Then her hatin'-ass friends cock-blocked with some shit about another party. And you went back to that house on Quincy Street you called home only to find the people that lived there—your parents, angels who'd brought about your salvation—coming out in body bags.

Some crew of shooters had gotten the address wrong. Your mom took a ricochet to the dome and died instantly. Pops went beserk and tried to box the men with the pistols. He ended up on the floor with as many holes in him as your real dad. Of course the cops had no lead on the perpetrators.

A couple weeks later, a grandma you'd never met showed up to pack up the place. There was no will listing you as next of kin, and your eighteenth birthday had already passed. So she gave you a month to get out.

You guessed that the kingdom of Heaven didn't last forever after all, that your time in the garden had to end, even if you'd played by the rules, even if you'd become something normal and respectable. In a week you dug up some of your old peoples, scattered associates from the group home days and the old neighborhood who you kept in just enough touch with.

You split open vanilla Dutch's and lined them with bits of green trees, lit, and inhaled. You drank Hen like water. You went back to school and did just enough to get by. Somewhere in the middle of that cloud your scholarship went *poof* and the registrar's office had its hand out. You had to pay to play for your education, and your pockets were on E.

So you took a job as a courier. The one thing Evil Grandma had let you keep was the old car, the '78 Range. So you put it to use, delivering packages and taking signatures, drinking coffee to come off the highs that stretched from night into the afternoon. The pay was barely enough for the room you rented in East New York. And you'd taken out a big loan to get through the rest of your sophomore year.

Then Fate brought you down from purgatory into Tony Star's den. You delivered a thick envelope to his address and asked for his signature. Just after he signed, he looked at your face and saw something in it he remembered from a long time before, something that reminded him of a man you would rather have forgotten. Tony Star had been your father's partner in that sham of a church long ago. The voice in your head told you that he'd had something do with his murder too.

Your whole story spilled into his ears while he was paying for the drinks. Maybe it was pity, or guilt, or something else, that made him put you on the payroll as an errand boy. A few months later you graduated to bagman, where you stayed, happily and peacefully until tonight, when your dick's gotten the best of you.

You should have known better. You got to the top of the world and then plunged beneath the sea. Now you're just trying to hold on, trying to maintain your grip on a slippery edge so you can start climbing again.

3.

There's a parking space right at the corner of Lafayette and Bedford. It's the perfect size for a monster truck like yours. After a night of the Devil's work, you're starting to believe in God again. There's a cool breeze whirling across Lafayette Gardens, coming from the river at just the right time, like rain to scorched soil.

A man the age your father would have been is rocking to a cassette Walkman and a pair of headphones from the WKRP era. It sounds like he's singing "Just Hangin' Out" by Main Source but he's a little too old for that. Maybe it's something else with the same beat.

You know the faces in this place because you used to live here, long before your good little life north of Gates. You know that elevator 2 always smells like piss, and that that nigga from the eighth floor is always up on the roof blowing trees and playing that same Mobb Deep tape out of his old-ass boombox. He's been doing it since '95. Why stop now?

Sometimes you feel like a stranger when you come here. Other times it's like you never left, like you only just came through that exit door with your bag packed and social worker in tow, on your way to that first group home, the one on Dean over by the Armory.

It seemed like they were all out there that day, waving you goodbye, the Johnsons and the Smiths, Candra and Chassity, and of course Chief, Will, and Mike Mike, your muthafuckas. Mike Mike actually shed a tear cuz he didn't want you to go. The others knew you'd be back, cuz that was "where you belong," they said.

But to tell the truth, you'd never been so sure about that. Even in the middle of all the dirt your peoples were into, you couldn't help feeling like your destiny was elsewhere. You got sick of getting cut by the glass on the playground. You got sick of all the fuckin' gunfire at night and looking down into the courtyard to see who'd just gotten dropped. You'd wanted out even as a little kid. But when you got out you kept coming back around, cuz it was the only place where the people understood you.

Now you're back here again, bruised and beaten and broken as you head from floor one up to five, the lift smelling more pissy than usual, like some kids were in there trying to see if they could leave enough for the roaches to swim in. And it's that yellow piss, that rancid kind from drinking nothing but carbonated sugar and liquor. At least the ride up is quick. You can still see the faded letters on the elevator ceiling, the initials your daddy lifted you up to write when you were like five, a *D* for both of you that would never fade away.

The doors open and close. You turn left and pass five doorways before you put a fist to 5G. It only takes a second before the door comes open and Chief is standing there, smelling like ketchup and hot sauce as he sucks down the last of a chicken wing covered in that stuff, the reason for all that gut he's got in the middle these days.

"Goddamn, nigga! They fucked you up good!" he says, way too loudly. You tell him to tell you some shit you *don't* know.

As usual the place is a pigsty: dirty clothes and old takeout bags, boxes, and cartons wherever you look. You follow him past the pile of laundry that's most likely been there, in the same place, since your last visit a month before. Trash cans are filled to the brim with VHS porno box covers and shredded paper. You don't know how the fuck he lives amongst all of this. But when you follow him down the short hallway and past the first bedroom where his mother sleeps to the one where he lays his own head, you see that it ain't all bad.

For the life of you, you can't figure out how a five-ten, 200-plus dude manages to sleep on a twin bed in the middle of his room, surrounded by the humming of machines and an accelerated broadband connection, equipment he assembled with his own hands from the money he put away while he was doing a bid down in Louisiana.

He got popped on some real dumb shit, playing errand boy for some wannabe gunrunner who said way too much on the land line. He got Chief to drive down there in a ride that turned out to be boosted to pick up about thirty pistols in a box and bring them back to Brooklyn. But since this dumb nigga he was working for was all but broadcasting his master plan, the Feds were waiting for Chief at the meet, the guns already in their possession. When it was all over they hit him with three and made him do the time down South somewhere, in some shithole Fed lockup nobody you knew had ever heard of. You couldn't even get mail to the place because it always got returned.

So he ended up serving three in a spot where there wasn't shit to do but get shanked, sodomized, or smothered to death by the humidity. But Chief being Chief had the gods smiling on him. He got cool with the prison computer tech who happened to loosely know one of the dudes on his cellblock. Some kind of way he gets this guy to bring him all these books on computers, networking, satellite shit, etc., and he basically teaches himself everything there is to know about computers.

Right before he went in, he took two grand he'd won in some gambling spot over on Putnam and bought himself a chunk of medical stock that quintupled in value while he was inside. So when he got released he cashed out, bought all the equipment he needed, and then moved back into the projects with his moms. All of this leads to one big point: If the info is out there, Chief can find it for you. And you know exactly who you need to find.

You ask him if he has anything for your ribs and he hands you a prescription bottle with a name you can't even spell. You swallow four instead of the recommended two and chase it with a beer and the last chicken wing in a styrofoam box on the table. There's no logical explanation for why your stomach lets you get away with that kind of shit.

"You know this is a shot in the dark, right?" he asks you, as he pushes a lime into a freshly opened Corona.

You tell him you have to take every shot in the

clip. He gives this sad nod, seeming to understand. He knows how deep you are in the shit.

"Son, now I ain't gonna say I told you so," he sighs. "But on the real, I told you so."

Chief was the first person who ever told you a story about Star. The loudmouth boss who'd gotten him busted had apparently had some dealings with him back in the day. When it was over, Tony went home with somebody's index finger in his pocket and the deed to the liquor store that the newly nine-fingered man had owned. The place went up in flames a month later because of a "gas leak," just after a $200,000 policy had been taken out on the place.

"This ain't the kinda nigga for you to be in the mix with," he said, rubbing the scarified mark on his forehead, the one his father had made with a knife when he was a baby as part of Hausa tradition. You call him Chief because that's what his name means in Hausa. Funny thing is that his mama is Native American. So it's like his dad named him some shit that's a stereotype for the other side of his heritage.

You tell your friend that now ain't the time for chastising, that all you can do is try and salvage this thing and stay alive long enough to find a way out of the job. You tell him everything: the money, the brown leather shoulder bag it was in, the perfume she wore, the tattoo at the small of her back, etc., any and everything you think might give him something to go with. He sits at the keyboard and jumps through a series of screens and search engines. Codes you don't understand all over the place.

"Nuthin'. I mean, who's gonna send a text of an e-mail that says, *I've got 200 Gs in a bag and I'm at this address.*"

You tell him he's got a point and then you try and think. Where can you find a trail? You don't even know this broad's real name. And as for the bartender, how the fuck you gonna remember what some dude serving up Hennessy is supposed to look like?

Then it hits you strangely and suddenly. Of course you don't know them. But management does. They have to have a record of their employees with the kind of dough that goes through there. Any theft in that club is always gonna be assumed to be an inside job.

You run the idea by Chief and it brings a grin to his face. "Now that's some shit we can do."

He punches in the name of the spot and pulls up an address. With that address he hacks into the phone company's records and gets an IP address for the place's security server. It takes a few minutes for him to crack the password protection but he gets in. He always gets in.

Carolina Martinez. Age twenty-two, five-four, 125 pounds. Her picture doesn't do her justice. Just seeing her face reminds you of the way she was looking up at you as she sucked you off, the sway of those perfect titties compressed in that bra custom made to get your money. The address is on Bedford Avenue off of Kosciuszko, less than a ten-minute drive from where you are.

More files come up. There are three bartenders and one is white. So you scratch him, because knowing Star's pro-black stance in everything, he would've said "white boy bartender." One of the dudes is six-three and around 220. The other's five-seven and 180. You've never seen a tall guy behind the bar on your pickup days so you assume he's the one, David Nickens, who lives in Flatbush on Empire and New York Avenue. The girl's closer.

"You sure these are the two?"

You tell him no, but you've got to start somewhere. He gives you the hard copies of all three profiles and then cuts the connection.

"You want me to roll with you?" he asks. Of course you don't want to do this alone. You ain't the kinda muthafucka to be kicking in doors and hunting down the kind of cash people kill for.

You've got cracked ribs and a whole lot more wear-and-tear than most of the boys you go to school with have ever taken. You need somebody to have your back.

But at the same time, if shit goes wrong and you come up empty (which playing the averages is more likely to happen), the last thing you want to do is bring somebody from the neighborhood down with you. Besides, Chief ain't no killer either.

You tell him not to worry, that you'll be all right, but to keep his phone close just in case. He pulls you into the half-hug that black men made famous and you're back in the pissy elevator a minute later heading toward the street. You didn't tell him where you were heading next because you think he'll disapprove.

It's a little after 11 when you get back to the ride, which is luckily just the way you left it. It occurs to you then that Star's boys might be tailing you some kind of way. But in your mind that can only be of help if you get into a jam. If they show up in the middle of things, they'll either be your backup or decoys to take the slugs in your stead.

You turn the key and head about eight blocks in the other direction, not far from Marcy. Will's crib is a few blocks north of there. You just hope he's home. But then again he's in a wheelchair. He's always fuckin' home.

Will is the other third of your surviving trio, the other man that was right beside you that night at Skate City. It was that night that put him in the wheelchair and his best friend, Mike Mike, in a coffin.

Unlike Chief, Will got out of the projects the first chance he got. Even though he was paralyzed he got a desk job working for the cops. Said he wanted to be somewhere that was trying to make things better. So he made copies, answered phones, and spent a whole lot of time hanging with the weapons guys learning about guns.

You personally think it was because he couldn't really fight anymore. Before Skate City, that nigga could outbox anybody. Big or little, cock-D or skin-and-bones, they all went down on the other end of his fists of fury. So when there were no more legs, no bouncing from one foot to the other in a boxing stance, you think he got hooked on this idea of taking down his enemies with something a little more expedient, even though there were no enemies anymore, at least not until now.

That's right, you're heading to Will's for hardware, some shit to wrap your trigger around just in case it gets too hot, just in case the bitch and the bartender won't give the dough up willingly. Damn. It's crazy that you're even thinking like this. You weren't that dude. Will was. You were the one who thought things out, who tried to squash the beefs, and here you are chasing after silhouettes in the shadows.

Will had also been the other one to tell you that Tony Star was not a man to get in the mix with, that he used people and left back on the corners where he found them. You told him that you knew what you were doing, and he laughed with those crooked-ass teeth of his.

"Not when it comes to this you don't," he said. "You ain't in the street like that."

He was right. You'd never stomped a nigga out just because. You'd only fired a pistol on that range out in Jones Beach. And that was when your foster dad took you there back in high school, just a few months before he got killed. Truth is, you aren't the least prepared for what the night demands.

The craziest thing about Will's life now is that he only lives a few blocks over from that first group home you lived in on Classon. It's a little house, not even a brownstone, but he owns it. He got it with a grant from the state for disabled entrepreneurs, a grant he flipped into a mail-order replica jewelry business. If you want cut glass to look like ice and steel, to look like platinum, then all your gotta do is hit up his website. Tons of ballers give Will business, men who are smart enough to keep their real things hidden.

You park just a few blocks from Armstrong and make your way across to his address. You can see the light on in the front window. He's waiting for you.

"And look at this big-head muthafucka!" he says with a smile as you embrace. His biceps bulge with every movement. He still lifts, still trains. Still keeps his hair cut low because he hates being a dark-skinned nigga with straight hair. "Something real bitch-made about it," he used to say.

"Damn, man, I ain't seen you in a minute." You tell him you've been busy with school. And that you're still running around for Star a lot. But that ain't the real truth. Truth is, you've never gotten over seeing him in that fuckin' chair, wheeling around the damn crib like something out of the Special Olympics. You still blame yourself. You still think you could've saved him somehow.

"You fuckin' wit' that same bitch?" he asks, referring to Rachel, the fudge-colored girl with the legs to die for. Big brown eyes and an IQ of 138. Not your usual type but it was fun while it lasted. You used to bring her everywhere, take her little boy out to the park and push him on the swings. Smoke out with her and fuck high on the couch after the two of you read him a bedtime story.

Problem was that she wanted you to be there all the time, for the sun to rise and set with the two of you together. And that shit was just too much, especially then. Both sets of your parents had died violent deaths. You felt like it was your fault, that you were the jinx that always brought the house down.

You remember the last time you made love to her, before you went to the Promenade to see the sun set. You never figured that was gonna be the last night. You never figured it'd be your own pride that would ruin it.

It was after all that that you ended up at the club so much, trying to drown all the fucked-up thoughts in your head by renting body parts from the bitch that's now got your life on the line. You call Rachel sometimes, only to hang up. You talk to her in your dreams and tell her you're sorry. But you ain't man enough to do any more than that.

"So what's the deal, man?" Will prods. "I know this ain't no social call on a Thursday night." You're happy that he's making it easy. Maybe he won't ask too many questions. Then you'll be in and out and on your way, without more guilt than you've already got.

You tell him you gotta tool up. His expression almost immediately turns to stone. Then there's a two-second pause before he answers.

"You fuckin' wit' me, right?"

You tell him that you wish you were, but you're in a situation where you ain't got a choice. He asks if you're in trouble and you don't lie. You tell him everything.

How the fuck could you ever lie to Will?

He saved your ass from beatdowns and a few bullshit run-ins with the cops when they almost caught y'all smoking on the corner. He was the one who showed you how to roll, the one who sealed the deal on your first piece of pussy by just telling the girl that you were a friend of his.

He had that kind of power over women: getting girls to strip down and pose on the sofa in his living room while you all watched, fuckin' chicks two at a time when he was he was still in high school. He was a something you could never be. And maybe in the end that wasn't altogether a bad thing.

"I ain't gonna say I told you so, but c'mon, son. You can't do this shit on the solo. You ain't that nigga. I'm that nigga but you ain't. Let me roll wit' you."

You have that same pause you had at Chief's crib just a few minutes earlier. That moment where "all right" is dangling on the tip of your tongue. But then you look at the wheelchair and that keloid scar on his shoulder. Then you know you can't do it again.

You tell him that you have to see this shit through alone, that Star has people tailing you, that they'll come in for backup if it gets rougher than you can handle.

He gives you that look like he doesn't believe you, but then gives you a nod anyway. "So whatchu want?"

You ask him what you can afford and he pats you on the shoulder, from a seated position, and tells you that it's on him, that it's the least he can do. Something bothers you about the look he gives you, but you can't put your finger on what it is.

"You know where the stash is," he says. "Down the stairs behind the door."

You ask him why he's looking at you like that, like there's something he wants to say.

"You know."

No, you don't.

"You know what this shit means, right?"

You tell him to get to the point.

"You go down dem steps and you turn into somethin' else. All that college-boy shit is over.

You pick up that heat and you on your way to being another muthafucka, a whole different nigga than who you was plannin' on bein'."

Something about the way he says the words scares you, like he's been to the place you're headed. And when you think about it in that moment, you know that he has.

He's telling you this because he loves you like a brother, because he doesn't want you to come back in the morning or next month or next year with that same chunk of your soul missing for life, the chunk that separates you from all the bodies out in the street that ain't got nothing to lose, no focus other than satisfying their silly little desires, no belief in anything other than money, pussy, and revenge.

The two of you look at each other for a long time. It's like the stereo goes on mute, like the little TV in the corner is turned off instead of on. No matter what happens tonight, something tells you that shit ain't gonna be the same between you two. So you better take the favor while it's there.

"I'll keep all that in mind," you say coldly, as you start down the short stairs to the basement, his eyes burning a hole in your back.

Will's armory is a walk-in closest in the guest room downstairs. He's got two Mossbergs hanging on the wall rack, about ten nine-millimeters, three .380s (one of them chromed), and a semiautomatic rifle with a scope you've never seen before. Rounds are in the toolbox on the floor.

If you knew anything about guns you'd go for the Glock or the Sig P226. They're both light with good reps and great reviews. Both are notorious for not jamming and have the least recoil of anything in the bunch. But in this life you don't know shit about guns, so you decide to go with something you've seen in a lot of movies: an M9 Beretta. Looks like that shit Bruce Willis had in *Die Hard*.

So that's what you go with, a heavy-ass four-pounder with three clips. You tuck it in the small of your back and the clips in your coat, turn the light out on the stash, and come back upstairs. Will's still right at the edge of the stairwell.

"What you go with, *killa?*" he asks.

You tell him.

"It's a lil' heavy," he says, grinning.

You tell him you can handle it, but ask why in the fuck does he have all of that artillery so out in the open? He tells you that they're all completely clean, batches he had a friend of his build with stolen parts, parts that had yet to get stamped with serial numbers. So basically they don't exist, not a one of them. And if there's no record of the thing, there's no tying them to any crime, unless there are fingerprints.

He suggests you find a pair of gloves or wipe it down real good after you use it. He also advises that the best place to dump it is a recycling center or a junkyard, somewhere the cops won't bother looking unless the body is a soul that happens to matter.

He hugs you as you tell him you have to get back on the trail. He says that you should think before you get any deeper into this mess, that maybe you should leave town. You tell him you're in school.

"That shit won't last after this," he says. "I guarantee it."

You leave Will and his wheels in the entrance doorway and let the screen door slap shut right in front of his face. You hate him for being honest. You hate him for giving you the gift of vision about how all of this is going to end. But you've got two addresses and an appropriate weapon. Ain't no turning back now.

You turn the radio up on your way to Flatbush. You figure the bartender's the less expected move. A broad like her would have cleared out her shit, would've known that the kind of men she stole from would be hot on her trail in no time, especially if Star already knew about it.

It's all a crapshoot anyway. Chances are, these

people are gone and you got hell to pay in the morning. And once the sun is up, one little nine ain't gonna save you against a gangster like Star. Shit, a fuckin' RPG wouldn't either. But you can't think about dawn yet. It's barely midnight. Maybe God will show his face in your life again. Maybe Will won't be right and you'll get out of this thing completely unscathed. Yeah, and Pac's *really* dead.

Every time you hit Empire Boulevard you think about the skating rink there, the *other* one with the reputation, the only one you know about besides Skate City. God, you keep thinking that shit. It's actually getting annoying. But for the purpose of the here-and-now, it's just a boulevard, just a street meant to lead you in the clear with the Devil just above your head.

The address brings you to a building on a hill. It's one of those big multi-unit joints that probably holds a couple hundred people, all those families connected by the same front door and mailboxes. You wonder what horrible things might go down if all the tenants knew there was somebody in there with a bag full of six figures in green.

You park at the bottom of the hill and hike back up on the opposite side of the street to the bus stop. You pose there, looking like just another lame soul catching the bus home with all the other lames who can't afford cars or the price of parking in the city.

David Nickens. Thirty-four years old. Two years on Rikers for gun possession. Apartment 2G, in the rear of the building. Going through the front isn't a problem, but getting past the apartment door is. One shell from a heavy hitter and you're in a body bag.

But the rear has its problems too. Even if there's a fire escape you've got to hope it's attached to the unit you need to be in. Besides, you ain't Batman. Climbing up some fire escape is the perfect way for you to bust your ass, have your tailbone in a sling, or some equally dumb shit. Then you get an idea.

It's real textbook, but just silly enough to work if somebody takes the bait. You open up your cell and dial the number of the Chinese takeout joint on the corner. You know it by heart because Star owns it. It's a drop spot for all of his captains, a place where all their people leave dough for them. The Korean guy (who actually went to Cornell but gets paid to sound like an immigrant) answers and takes the delivery order for fried shrimp and a quart of pork fried rice. Since it's near closing time you figure they'll show up pretty fast.

You'll make it a point to be somewhere near the entrance door when the delivery guy comes in. Even if Nickens sends them away, he'll still think it's the delivery guy if he gets a knock on the door. If he accepts the food and lets them up, you follow them in from a distance and catch your boy with his pants down. It ain't the best plan. He may not be there at all, or you could miss the door, or it could be any number of mishaps. But it's the best you can come up with so you're gonna go for it.

You light your first smoke of the evening and breathe freely as Chief's painkillers start to kick in. The soreness eases on either side of you and the nicotine makes everything else follow suit. You watch a choice ass thump past you, as well as a few cop cruisers, mostly on their way over to The Stuy or somewhere in that direction. It's cool enough outside to feel comfortable, but warm enough that your bones don't get that chill.

It's just after midnight when some Korean kid who looks about fifteen comes biking up the hill to the designated address. You jog across the street and post up by one of the pillars next to the first unlocked entrance door. He comes up clueless, stares at the piece of paper where the number's written, and hits apartment 2G.

There's no answer at first. So he waits a few

seconds, tries again. Nothing still. He's about to ring for a third time when a voice crackles over the intercom.

"Yeah?" Nickens (or who you assume is Nickens) asks. His voice is soft and real effeminate, but you know it's dude, and he seems to be in a rush. The Lord is with you after all.

"You order Chinese food?"

"No, I didn't. Wrong apartment."

"But I have the number right here."

You know this is going to go back and forth like some kind of a comedy routine for the next minute or so, a minute you take to squeeze into the first unlocked entrance door. And once you do, you find that, to your surprise, the second door is unlocked as well. 2G. 2G. All you have to do is get to 2G.

You start up the stairs, treading lightly but quickly. You don't want your shoes to squeak on the linoleum. Come up to the door and knock, get the fuck outta the frame, wait for him to unlock it, then you kick him to the floor. Yeah, that'll work. You just have to concentrate. And your timing has to be perfect. That's all it is. Perfect timing and this will be over with soon.

You pass 2B and 2D and stay to the right until you see that G is going to be on the left. The halls are empty. Good. No kids to get in the way. No witnesses. No nothing. You grab the butt of your pistol and flip the safety off. He should've sent Chinese delivery boy home by now.

You get that weak feeling in your hands again. Your heart is racing. You feel beads of sweat forming at the back of your neck. You can't fuck this up. You cannot fuck this up. You cannot fuck this up. You say it over and over inside your brain, hoping that it will get you out of Oz.

You turn to face the doorway with gun in hand and are just reaching for the bell when the door comes open right in front of you. You're face to face with the dude who you came to see. Nickens the bartender is right there, right in front of you, with your bag, the same fuckin' bag that was sitting next to you hours before, slung over his shoulder. Carolina Martinez is directly behind him. And behind them both is a nigga the size of two refrigerators. This is the moment that Will was just talking about, the one that will tell you exactly who you are.

You raise your weapon, aim dead at the money man in front of you, and say something straight out of a movie. "Let's take a walk back inside." One eye is locked on Nickens, the other on the giant dude behind him. But you're not watching the girl. You're not keeping track of the bitch who started this fuckin' thing, the one who ruined your whole fuckin' night. And that is your mistake.

She fires a shot from under the bartender's arm that barely misses your shoulder. You fire back without aiming and somehow manage to put a hole in Nickens's skull the size of a C-battery. He drops to the floor and you fire into the bigger man, who falls backwards, but you don't see blood so you assume he's wearing a vest. You know he'll be back up as soon as the pain wears away.

The bitch is struggling to pull the bag out from under her dead partner-in-crime when you slap her across the face with the front of end of your pistol and mush her to the floor with your free hand. There are screams behind you in the hallway. And if there are the screams, somebody's dialing 911. You grab the bag and head for the stairwell, knowing that you can't go out the front. The cops might already be there.

So you do a 180 at the bottom of the landing and start looking for another way out. There's an alarmed emergency exit at the other end of the building. You unzip the bag enough to see money and you keep tracking for the door.

When you get to it you kick it open and the alarm comes on, high school fire-drill style.

Next thing you know, you're running down a thin strip of concrete into an alley. You cut right and head for the next street and then make another left onto another one, where you stop. You have to stop. Nobody's behind you. You have to stop acting like you're being chased. All you gotta do is get back to the car. Get back to the car. Get back to Star. Get back to class tomorrow afternoon. The shit should be real simple. But at least one person is dead already, and you killed him. And that's the least simple shit you've ever dealt with in your twenty-four years.

You make a smooth beeline back toward your ride. It takes a few minutes for you to find it with all of the twists and turns, but it's right there, right beyond the yellow tape the cops are already using to close off the street.

You put the bag on the floor beneath your feet as you pull out your key. The ignition stalls for a moment before turning over, making you think someone wired it with a bomb, that you're dead even after you got what you needed.

But then a new set of worries hit you. Were there any witnesses? Do the cops have a description? Did that bitch and the big man stick around long enough to give statements? Is there shredded paper in the rest of the bag? Did you snag a decoy and shoot the bartender and the big man before they could lead you to the real dough?

You can't turn your brain off and you keep seeing that hole in Nickens's head, that look of shock on his face that said this was the last way in the world he'd been planning on going out. Shit, think about it, he's out the door with the girl and the money and another nigga who has his back, only to get caught slippin' by the non-thug he took for more than 200 Gs just a few hours before. It's the worst kind of luck, far worse than your own.

You turn right on New York Avenue and head back toward The Stuy, using your free hand to dial Star's cell so he can call off the dogs. But there's no answer. You try again at the light at Eastern Parkway, and nothing still, which doesn't make sense. This is his direct line. It doesn't even go to voicemail even though he's got close to a quarter mil missing out on the street. Then you tell yourself to calm down. For all you know he's fuckin' one of those broads from the club, maybe the one who always wears the see-through g-strings, or the one you like with the micro-braids and the dragon tattooed on one of her little yellow breasts.

What you need to do in the meantime is lay low, find a place to hole up and get your bearings, check the TV to see if the cops are looking for you, and, most importantly, make sure that what you need is in the bag. You know of the perfect place, that flophouse on Myrtle Avenue you used to take girls to back when you still lived with your foster parents. It's open all night and you haven't been there since you started working for Star, so it's off his radar. Good move.

Then you start thinking about your ride. You've been all over in it, which makes it recognizable. Might be best to stash it and the dough until you hear from Star. After all, it's barely 1 a.m. and you've got until daybreak. Keep them both close enough for easy access, but away from any unseen eyes. You decide to leave the ride in short-term at JFK and then train it back to the neighborhood with the dough in tow. That should shake any tails.

You've always loved driving out Conduit Avenue. There's more room to open up and pick up speed, especially at this time of night, nothing but cabs and commercial trucks. You've made a couple runs this way for Star to get people here and there, usually zoning off a well-rolled L. You'd have Marvin in the deck, maybe some Biggie or Jagged Edge. Let your mind disappear between the median and broken lines. It calms you now, pushes what just happened into the background, makes the ambush of questions slowly begin to retreat.

Rachel was with you one time. She wasn't supposed to be but you were just going to get delayed luggage. That was the night she told you she loved you, when she unzipped your fly right after you shifted into fourth gear. You were doing close to seventy when she took it into her mouth, her braids smelling of that African Pride stuff she always put in them. Some dude in a tractor trailer rolled by you on the left, took in the scene, and thrusted an *ay-okay* finger sign out the window. But she didn't let you come. She made you save that for much later. She loved that mistress torture shit.

Short-term parking is all but deserted. After all, only red eyes are still coming in this time of night. You put your ride close to the exit and hop out. Then you start the long walk from the lot to the bus that connects to the subway.

You're itching to open the bag again on the train ride back, but you refuse to take the risk. All you need is for some set of punks to get a whiff of cash and you may have to finish out that clip you've got. Better to pretend like its socks and underwear, some jeans and maybe a book you had for the plane. That's what anyone watching you heading in this direction is going to expect—that you're just some pathetic college kid who can't afford a cab.

You get off at Broadway Junction to switch to the J. It takes a half hour for a train to crawl in and almost another half for it to move you five stops to Myrtle and Wyckoff. Bushwick is all but dead at this time of night, though you can hear the faint sounds of salsa from an open window somewhere. A man twice your age walks by speaking Spanish into a cellphone, something about missing her. Why the fuck were those words the ones you had to translate?

Will is a fuckin' jinx. You haven't thought about the girl in forever and now she's all over the place, whispering all the choice memories to you like some kind of phantom, even though she's alive and well and most likely giving some other man the pleasures that you used to partake in. You hate Will for being right twice. He said you were a real dumbass for letting her go.

You hop a gypsy cab to the Louissaint Motel. Fifteen dollars for an hour. They ring the phone when time is up. When the fuck did it ever take an hour back in high school?

Harold, the owner, is a tall man with a receding hairline. He bought the joint at some tax auction back in the '80s and has half his family living in the place. The free rooms give him a little extra cash and the opportunity to peddle trees and X to the guests. As with all hotels, it's the accoutrements that make him his real money.

"Been a long time," he says to you, even though you thought he wouldn't recognize you with the baldie and goatee.

You nod. "Got some company on the way?"

"Maybe," you say as you start toward the elevator.

The whole spot is even more of shithole now than it was a few years before. Some joker has turned the walls of the entire floor into one long piece of graffiti. The brown carpet is worn and patchy. Entire chunks have been yanked out. You've got a little too much class for this kind of thing. You've upped your game a bit. And that's a good thing.

It's also good that the deadbolt on the room door works, even though the marks and splintering on the back of it say that it's been changed more than once. The bed feels like two slabs of a wood with a layer of cotton balls between them, the kind of piece that might literally blow a broad's back out.

But it's okay to sit on. You turn on the click-dial TV and the news is all but over with. You'll have to wait until the rerun in an hour or two if you want to see whether you're on the most wanted list. You let out a yawn as you open the bag and dump the cash on the table. You did a quick count before but you want to make sure. Forty minutes and two counts later it's miraculously all there, which confuses you even more.

Shouldn't at least a little be missing, enough for

some Cristal or a cab ride, a little taste for any other accomplices who might have been waiting in the wings? But it's all there, down to the last dollar. Maybe they were on their way to split it up. But if that was the case, what were they doing in the three hours you were out of the picture?

Had they been waiting for something? Instructions from someone else? A third party who was owed a piece of the loot? Where had the big man come from and why did it seem like he wasn't holding when the shootout started?

You can't get all the loose ends out of your head, even if they should no longer concern you. You've got the dough. Your role in all of this is over and done with once you get the bag back to the man it belongs to.

You try Star again but the phone just rings. It's been almost three hours and he hasn't as much as checked in with you. No voicemail might make sense. As a crime lord, do you really want people leaving you messages that might be checked remotely? But why the fuck isn't he answering? And what the fuck does that mean for you?

You're putting the rubber-banded stacks back in the bag when the local news re-airs. The shooting makes the first five minutes but there's no description of the perp and no witnesses. They don't even give Nickens's name since his family hasn't been notified. It seems as if you're still in the clear as long as the cops don't come across the nine you emptied. You'll need to get rid of it soon, and there's something about the whole recycling center thing that you just don't buy.

You check the clip. Ten rounds left, plus you have two extra clips. Until you find Star you have to assume that you're still a target, even if you're not in his crosshairs. Just then you're cell goes off. Star finally?

"You straight man?" It's Chief. He sounds worried about you.

You tell him you're lovely.

"Good. You got that thing?"

You tell him not to trip, that everything is all right in the world and that you're enjoying life. He asks you where you are and you tell him that you're cool, that you're just waiting to hear from you-know-who.

"Righteous, son, righteous," he replies.

Something about hearing him say that makes you feel better. If your boy's at ease then you should be too. But this Star thing is still bothering you. You want to bring it all to a close before the painkillers wear off. And if you're gonna do that, you'll have to go to the club.

But should you keep walking around with this kind of dough? You should stash it somewhere else until you can pinpoint Tony. Then you can take him back to that spot so that he can get his hands on it himself. But where can you stash that kind of dough and feel okay about it? The answer is a place you told yourself you'd never return to.

No one lives at your foster parents' old house. When the old lady tried to sell it, you got a lawyer and hit her with a cease-and-desist that has the whole thing tied up in court for at least another six months. Phone and lights are long gone. But your foster father's box is still there, right under the deck stairs that lead out into the backyard.

Funny thing is that he used to keep his hunting rifles there. Him and a few of his boys would go upstate once a year and take shots at deer. One time he came back with so much meat that you were all eating venison for three weeks straight. That shit was good though, cooked so soft and meaty that it came right off the bone. You used to chop it up and mix it with scrambled eggs, cheese, onions, and cilantro and call it breakfast. The good days. Days long gone.

You have a car service pick you up a few blocks from the motel, just in case someone's watching. It's that kind of late-at-night where there's nothing on Myrtle but cabs. Yours, #246, reeks of that sweet strawberry incense that makes you nauseous. You study the driver's eyes in the rearview mirror, trying to figure out if he's gay. Only a fag would burn that kind of shit. Or maybe it's his broad's idea. Who knows?

It's a short ride back up to the old house. The whole block is a corpse. All those white folks that moved in have work in the morning. The niggas who are left weren't the type the cop squads were looking to clean out. Nice morally upright people with plans for the future. Just like your second set of folks, before those assholes peeled them off the face of the earth.

Whoever they were, they came and went without a trace, which was kind of a mystery in a hood where somebody knew something about everything. You told yourself that maybe they were out-of-towners, hitmen who someone had farmed in, then back out again the minute the job got botched. The intended bastards are probably still in the same place they were those two years ago, sitting in rocking chairs whistling, never knowing that two perfect strangers caught the bullets with their names on them.

There had been times when you thought about hunting the guys down, looking for leads like you were some kind of private eye, asking questions in bars and on street corners like somebody was

actually gonna give up something real. You
always told yourself it wasn't worth it, that
vengeance was the Lord's and all that. Then you
killed a man over a bag of money that ain't even
yours.

The latch on the front gate still sticks,
something you were supposed to fix back when
they were still breathing. You make your walk
around to the back and find the rusty box with
the lock on it. Combo is still the same. 6-4-6. It
springs open like a hanging jaw, the heavier
bottom half swinging back and forth. It's
completely empty.

You were kind of hoping there might still be
some remnants of them: pictures, a note to you,
something the old bag might have missed. You
remember once hearing something about her
leaving her car running for like three days, right
in front of her own house. But you're sure she got
ahold of all the jewels and cash you didn't put the
freeze on with that lawsuit.

It's fucked up how when people die they
become nothing but their possessions, which get
argued over and divied up like spoils of some war.
The old broad just appeared one morning with a
big-ass truck and started boxing shit up like it
was all hers. Was she gonna fence the shit or
what? From what you'd heard, she lived in some

retirement home in Jersey. So it was probably all going on the auction block.

You stuff the bag into the box and then close it back up, and you're outta there. You can't stay there too long. Nothing worse than remembering Heaven in Hell. You hoof it up to Franklin and flag another car. Time to get back over to Star's.

4.

You see the funniest thing driving up Franklin to Fulton. Well, it ain't funny exactly. But it's the kind of real shit that lets you know the Brooklyn you came up in still exists. There's some Asian dude standing outside of a bodega wearing a bicycle helmet of all things. And it looks like he's arguing with a dude about twice his size, some black/latino hybrid with a serious fuckin' attitude.

Now, the very fact that this dude is in front of that bodega next to the train station at this time of the morning, on a block notorious for hookers, dealers, and zombie traffic all at once, is a freak of nature in itself. You can remember when niggas used to hang out over there just to jump cornballs coming out the train for exercise. They tried to catch you like that once, but a cop of all things got in the way. The next day you came over there with every dude from the gardens who you and Will could put together, just to let 'em know that you never walked alone.

So now this dude is out there, most likely a little too far from the renovated crib he just bought west of Classon, which is the line between occupied Bed-Stuy (which they now call Clinton Hill so that white folks moving in over there won't get nervous) and what is, has, and will hopefully always be the rest of the place you call home.

But okay, so this yellow man is over here on the other side of the world, and now he gets into some beef with a black man in a hoodie and jeans at 3:00 in the morning. What argument could he possibly win with this dude? What could possibly be worth losing permanent teeth? Even you, with two years of college under your belt, can't figure it out.

The punch crushes the guy's face like a soda can. You only get a quick glance as your taxi drives by, but you know that the stomping will soon commence, followed by even more ugly actions. Some of those other dudes on the corner could jump in. His bike may be for grabs. They might remove his helmet only to beat him with it. They will tear him apart like wild hyenas, not only because they can, but because they *have to*.

For most brothers the blocks are all they know, the only thing that defines them. What is life if they can't get four chicken wings and fries for the same price rain or shine? What good is it if more than a few of them haven't hit off the same broad so they can call her a ho for not being stupid enough to settle down with them? And how can you hold your head high in a neighborhood full of your own people if you let some punk-ass Asian punk you in front of your fellow neighbors?

The college-educated man on the ground doesn't understand any of this. He lives in an America where he has a right to an opinion and a right to prove it to someone else. To him, arguing is part of his civil rights, part of what it means to be living in the land of the free, enjoying life, liberty, and the pursuit of property.

A Long Island Railroad train rockets onto an elevated track from an underground tunnel, heading for the Nostrand Avenue station. Rachel used to take that out to Hempstead, back when she worked in the admissions office at Hofstra. Sometimes you'd go out there to see her. Grab a burger in the cafeteria and look at all the broads you wouldn't be fuckin'. The one thing you like about yourself is that you've never been a cheater. You always stuck it out no matter how crazy shit got, no matter how fast things ran into the ground.

You hop out of the cab at Utica still feeling paranoid, still wondering if eyes are on you somehow. You double back to Stuyvesant. It's a little bit of a hike but you figure you'll notice tailing cars better on foot.

An owl hoots somewhere as the club comes into view. Star told you that it was the first piece of property he ever bought, back in the '80s when you could buy a building in these parts for like five dollars. Said he wanted to have a place for dudes like him, where you didn't have to dress up to get a good drink and hear music, where undercovers got sniffed out the minute they came on the scene and all that. According to him, it's never been much of a moneymaker. But it's always been a home. And that's far more important.

It's just after 3:30 when you get to the front of the place to find that the lights are on and the gates are up, which takes you by surprise since they're supposed to shut down at 2 by law. You try the door and it opens like it's 6 in the evening. Something is very very wrong.

You know how wrong it is when you cross that threshold, when that dude you kicked in the nuts is missing half his torso in a pool of blood right in front of you. Your foot touches a rib fragment caked in fresh blood. More red stuff is splattered all over the liquor stash. You peer over to see that Wilfred, the old barman who's been working there since before he lost a leg to diabetes, has a hole in the right side of his head. It appears that the sawed-off in his hands has been fired once. From the looks of things, it tore that framed photo of dogs playing poker to shreds.

The register is closed shut and the key's not in the slot, which means that it's most likely in the late Wilfred's pocket. Either way, you know this wasn't a robbery. The only two bodies are employees. No turned-over chairs. No signs of a struggle. Somebody just walked in and started letting off. Feels like they knew who they wanted and where to find them. And they knew Wilfred wouldn't be fast enough to stop them.

Or maybe they had the advantage of numbers. Three or four would have been more than enough to level any and all opposition. And if they came this far, you know they went up to the office. It's the only thing that would've made sense.

So you follow the trail, up those two flights of creaky stairs, past the floor full of office furniture that used to be open for dancing until the cabaret license got revoked.

You remember the time you saw your old friend Bink hurling in the entrance way after mixing Bacardi light and dark on a stomach full of nothing but salad (cuz he was trying to be a vegan that week). Come to think of it, that was right before he caught that gun charge. They gave him an extra two because it was his second strike. He'd been the last man out of some liquor store holdup in Fort Greene. Popped him right above the knee and he had a limp for life. But the store owner didn't ID him so the cops pushed the pistol thing to the limit.

You used to go and see him sometimes. You'd bring him books and shit, mostly graphic novels and porn, *Erotique Noire* and that *Dark Eros* book, sex shit that fucked with your mind, shit you could make last in a place with no pussy for a nigga who at six-six and 230 wasn't ever going the other way. Then one morning he just didn't wake up. Aneuryism in his fuckin' sleep. You'd only been around for a couple months when he crossed over. God must not have been looking out for him.

You keep up two more flights, pistol out, safety off. You try to count out the number of shots left in the clip. Ten, or is it twelve? Then you remind yourself again that you have two more clips and don't need to sweat it so much. You keep seeing that hole in Nickens's head though, and the way the big man went down.

There are still specs of dried blood on your shirt and jeans. You should have changed, burned all your clothes, showered, shaved, whatever the fuck would cut down on all the DNA. But there was no time. And now there's this quaking in your stomach that isn't good, different from the nausea from before, and you don't see it going away anytime soon.

The double doors that lead to Star's office are five feet away. Four. Three. Two. You kick them and both doors swing wild and fast, revealing four barrels pointed at your skull. One of them is held by the broad who had your cum down her throat just yesterday, then shot at you hours later. It's time for another frozen moment, another countdown to certain death.

Now here's what you know. You know that you've shot two members of this at least six-person crew and relieved them of the bag of cash they rightfully stole. You also know that they're obviously aware of who you work for, and since neither Star nor his corpse are anywhere to be found, you figure that he's alive somewhere, and if he's alive he not only still wants his money from you, but he also wants every gunman in front of you dead as steak in the supermarket as soon as humanly possible.

If you run they'll use you for target practice. But then again maybe they won't, since you still have the money and the money is what they must be here for. This gives you an advantage, at least you think it does. They need you and you need time to figure a way out of this.

Your girl does the talking. "I don't even have to say it, do I?" She arches her perfectly arched eyebrows for emphasis, titties forcing themselves through her low-cut shirt.

You know you can hit her, put an end to the bitch that started this whole fuckin' thing, have the satisfaction that she'll be headed to Hell just a few seconds before you. But you ain't got suicidal tendencies so you lower your weapon and leave it on the stair in front of you.

You're not even standing upright when the boot hits you in the face. You tumble backwards, rolling like a tire over rough terrain. Darkness again.

Your ribs wake you up sometime later, along with the taste of another broken tooth. You can feel the tiny bits of enamel all over your mouth. But at least there's no blood. That's always a plus. The clock on the wall is the first thing that comes into focus. It's pushing 4 in the morning.

You recognize the two bodies next to you almost immediately. Both were part of the muscle team that went to work on you right after you got got in the first place.

You glance across the room and get your first good look at the enemy. The big man you hit in the chest over in Flatbush is busy tearing into the file cabinets you know are full of nothing but invoices and tax returns for the bar. A skinny dude with a baldie and angel tattoo on his neck is fitting a bit into a drill in his lap, most likely meant for the safe hidden in the floor, the one everybody inside the Star unit knows is rumored to hold a million in cash.

Your bitch is rifling through the desk drawers. And the last man, a fake Vince Carter–looking muthafucka with Tims and baggy jeans has both eyes on you, his pistol less than a foot from your face.

"You don't try nuthin' and I don't cap nothin'," he says with a grin, chewing on gum that you can tell has already gone stale. He's biting down hard just to calm his nerves. You give him a nod that says you'll play ball. He gives you a nod that says he appreciates it.

You study each face one by one and they gradually become familiar. It didn't hit you earlier but you've seen the big man before. He works security at the Star Lounge on Nostrand. You figure he was the one who shot you in the alley before you shot him at Nickens's apartment. Kevlar's worth every penny. The guy with the baldie DJs there the nights you do your drop. Your babysitter is assistant manager at the other strip club on Snyder. He must have been wearing a vest too.

Bottom line is that they all work for Star. Even if it's shit, unimportant jobs, they're all on the payroll, and they all know that you're his bagman. A conspiracy is harder to trace if its members work at different, unrelated spots. You're the only bridge between them because of your route.

But what are they looking for? And where the fuck is Star? From what you know, he all but fucks with security around him. And if he got away, why hasn't he come back to blow them all to kingdom come?

"It ain't here!" the bitch says to rest of them, slamming the final desk drawer.

"Then where the fuck is it?" Big Man asks, as he pulls his massive fingers away from the files.

"I told you it wouldn't be," Baldie says. "I told you, we gotta drill into the box."

Looking at the drill, you get the impression this guy just took the price tag off of it. You're dealing with a crew of amateurs, even more amateur than you. They're searching for something they don't know how to find, and they've killed at least four people doing it, losing one man in the process thanks to you. You'd tell them all of this if your ribs weren't killing you and ol' boy to the left with the Desert Eagle wasn't looking for an excuse.

He's most likely their triggerman. He has that

look about him. Pulled a trigger once and it made him thirsty for more. You've heard about dudes like that, heard about the excuses they make to keep the local morticians in business—until their clock expires in a bloodier way than they punched all of the others.

"There's no time for that," the bitch says. "We gotta find this muthafucka before he figures out what we're doing."

"Are you kidding?" Baldie replies. "He'd never think it's—"

"A bunch of people who work for him," you interject.

They all freeze, as if they almost forgot you were sitting there. You continue.

"He might not yet, but it's only a matter of time."

"How the fuck you know who we work for?" the killer next to you asks.

"I know where you all work at," you say.

The killer presses the tool into your cheek until it hurts. "If you want to live, you'd keep that shit to yourself."

You keep it going, trying to make them nervous, trying to slip as much doubt between the bricks of their flimsy foundation. Then you realize that they haven't even tied you up or closed the double doors to the stairwell.

"As if I'm not gonna end up like these niggas next to me. Baldie's right. What you want is in the box. And you ain't even gotta drill it open. I got the combo."

"What are we looking for?" the bitch asks you, putting a hand to her lovely hip.

"The emergency stash in there. The million in hundreds he keeps on hand just in case."

They all look at each other for a moment. They're not there for the money, but the money might actually be better than what they came for.

"And how the fuck do you know about that?" Big Man chimes in. You're telling just enough truth to make the lies go down like honey.

"I'm like his nephew. He and my daddy used to do jobs together."

They all give each other these glances of both panic and interest. You could be their gold mine, their blueprint to robbing Star blind. Or you could be bait for a trap.

"He thought it was Nickens the whole time," you say. "That's why he sent me to his crib first. That's why I hit him and not y'all."

They look at each other and all start to grin.

"They really thought Dave was the fuckin' mastermind," Big Man laughs.

"Yeah, son was a fuckin' square on the

strength," Baldie adds. "We just thought you hit him to make an example."

You're starting to get into this whole acting thing. The stories come together in your mind like you actually saw them play out in front of your eyes. All you have to do is not get the details wrong from here on out and you're straight as an arrow.

"Nah, y'all are off the radar for now, long as you get out before he comes back—"

"Wait a minute," the bitch interrupts. "Why are you telling us all this?"

"Because I spent half the night running around trying to get that cash back to save my own ass from ending up like these dead niggas over here. If y'all are making a play for Star, you're solving my problem for me."

"But he's like your uncle, right?" the killer asks.

"I got a lot of uncles," you say.

The bitch gives you that seductive grin she usually saves for the VIP. "And I thought you was more square than Dave."

There's something inside of you that wants to see a hole through her head to match the bartender's. But you don't let it show. Now ain't the time for true colors. Your gun is tucked in back of Big Man's pants.

"Mama, I'm a lot of things you don't know about."

You'd like your words to make her cream, but you'll settle for a deep grin, which you get.

"So what do you want for the combo?"

"I just wanna live," you say, wincing at a sharp pain on your right side. You're afraid that the fall might have changed bruised to fractured, or fractured to broken, or whatever else might make bad go to worse. But as long as you keep the gab up and keep them interested, the pain won't matter so much. Especially after you give them the combo.

They are giving each other these looks, as if they're not exactly sure what to believe, but that what you're asking for doesn't seem to be too much. It's something they can live with. All you have to do is not make the mistake of asking too many questions, of prying too much into their master plan, and you just might get to walk out of here.

"Give us the combo. If what you say is in there is, we let you go. If not, you go where them two is headed."

You give them the numbers. Big Man, Baldie, and the bitch make their way to the corner of the room and start lifting the loose boards to get to the safe. Killer stays with you though, giving you that look that says he's gonna be cautious no matter what.

It's an old-school dial, one where you have to turn left, then right, and then pull the bar. Star told you it came with the place back when he bought it, and even he thought it was real old school to have a safe in the floor of his office. That was like some old Edward G. Robinson shit. If it all got too rough, you emptied it out and booked for the train station or the airport, or, worse come to worst, the broke-ass Port Authority. Start new somewhere else.

What you wouldn't do to start over now, to wind back the clock and make the drop the way you were supposed to. Had you done that, these muthafuckas around you would've still had day jobs, would've still been nothing but people punching a clock. You would've got your envelope, had a few drinks from Wilfred, and maybe met a piece of ass worth letting stay the night.

Now, as Baldie turns the dial, the proper settings at left and right and then left again, you have to brace yourself. There are two inches of cable running from the safe door to two thermite grenades superglued to half a cinder block at the mouth of the safe. You gave Star the idea when he first told you about the safe. Nice little failsafe in case of a robbery.

The blast blinds and deafens you all at once. Half of Big Man is covered in fire as he falls into the hole where the safe and floor used to be. The bitch is rolling around on the floor, trying to dampen the flame on her coat into submission. Killer sits next to you, frozen in disbelief.

You'd built the trap but never fully imagined the way it might be sprung. You'd put together the plan, but you never imagined it would work this well. Killer comes to his senses just as you do. He sprints at you wildly, leaving himself open and his most precious jewels unguarded. He gets a nice firm tap in the nuts before he even gets close. In three seconds he's curled up in a ball. You pry the gun from his hands and get ahold of your own. But just as you point it in the bitch's direction, you find that there's nothing left of her to speak of. She's gone.

You walk over to the edge of the crater where a fifth of the room used to be, and you see two flaming bodies smoldering on the storage level below. Good thing that wood's fire-proofed. Looking down at them, you almost forgot about the guy you just kicked in the nuts, the killer who's emptying his clip at you while you've got you back turned. Thinking flight instead of fight, you jump into the hole and fall a story, landing on the two corpses.

You glance up into Star's office but Killer isn't looking over the edge for you, which lets you know he ain't a complete idiot. But you can hear him coming down the stairwell, heading for the closed entrance door about six feet in front of you. You flip your safety off just as he kicks the door in. You don't give him a chance to fire as you let loose, landing three where his heart should be. He drops where he is, and that's that. You've now killed four people in six hours.

You get up and race past Killer and down the stairs. Last thing you want is to be caught here when the cops show up. But as you hear the patter of cheap leather on fire-treated wood, you know they've already beat you to the punch. You have just enough time to wipe the gun and clips clean and tuck them under a dust mop in the storage closet before somebody's slamming you into the framed picture of Lou Rawls.

The glass splinters but doesn't cut you. Instead, you melt to the floor like something out of a cartoon. Some pig clamps the bracelets on you while another one lifts you up by your neck. As your rights are read, you're trying to put together a story that will both keep you in the clear of everything that's happened and get you out of the precinct as soon as possible, which in Brooklyn is a minimum of six hours, featuring at least three interrogations, a thorough background check, and maybe, just maybe, a bit of police brutality. Sure, you don't know any of this from personal experience, but with more than your share of dogs in this life, you know what's fact and what's fiction.

You ask them what you're getting booked for and they don't answer, which is exactly what you want to hear. Right about now you're like that dude in *The Usual Suspects*, the only nigga breathing in a place filled with bodies. There's not a doubt in your mind that there's some boy in blue back at Star's spot whose job it is to find your prints on some shit they can hold over you head. That's why you dumped the gun in a damn closet under a mop. With all the pistols everywhere, fingering you as a triggerman is some murky shit. Your goal is to make it even murkier by playing up your role as the victim.

Of all the things in the world, the cop cruiser smells like patchouli. The pigs in question, a brother and a Puerto Rican, around the same height and build: solid but not buff, dense but not doughy. Off foot patrol but nowhere near their next promotion.

Surprisingly, they don't fuck with you, which means somebody told them you're a potential witness. If not, you imagine they'd be saying all kinds of shit to scare you, to make you wanna start snitching. Either they know something you don't or they're hoping you've got something they need. Anyway, these are good signs. Very good signs.

They take you to the 71st Precinct on Empire, not that far from the building where you put down the bartender. Thoughts of him bring back that smell of burning flesh up in Star's office after the grenades. Almost reminded you of rabbit or that Peking duck you and Rachel had down at the Chinatown festival that time you went. Shit was greasy but it was good. So good that she licked your fingers, even when it was her plate.

That was like date #6, wasn't it? She wasn't even your girl yet when you told her you had something you wanted to show her in the cab. You remember that sly grin she gave you as you undid her jeans and buried you fingers inside of her, flicking her clit back and forth with your thumb until she came with a hand over her mouth so the driver wouldn't know. She looked down at you with those big brown eyes of hers, completely in love. How the hell could you let her go?

The memory brings a clublike erection to your jeans as you're being led into Interview Room #3. The Puerto Rican cop pulls out the chair and you take a seat. The brother asks if you smoke. You tell him you do but you're not in the mood. And then they leave you there, still cuffed, to wait for whoever or whatever might be on the way.

You ask yourself questions that don't matter. How many people have been in this same chair in this same room? How many different people's blood might a forensics team find on the floor and walls herein? Why didn't you call Rachel after that night at Fort Greene Park? Why didn't you try to fix it instead of letting time wash it away like sand from a shoreline?

Looking back, it had been such a stupid argument to begin with. The two of you were there coolin' out on the benches watching all the people dance, black bodies swirling across the open space like 200 tornados colliding to the rhythm of deep house. She loved house and you loved her, so you came, even if you knew it would be full of all the earthy niggas and the fags and that clique of people you used to know during your ten seconds of wanting to be a rapper, a ten seconds that got you rapping right after the bridge of an R&B single that ended up getting shelved, some half-Mexican broad some A&R thought would be the next big thing.

So anyway, you were out there, her legs resting across your lap as you passed an L back and forth. She smelled like apples when you rubbed your nose against the back of her neck, smelling that oil in her hair, running your fingers along the creases on her scalp between the braids.

"What you thinkin' about?" she purred.

"You," you said. With her it wasn't a lie. With her it wasn't about smashin' and breakin' out.

"I'm glad you came wit' me. I know this ain't your thing."

"I'll go anywhere that got to do with you," you said back, feeling the blunt in your hand burning down to nothing.

"Then go out there with me," she said, pointing to the moving mass of people on the makeshift dance floor.

You didn't want to go out there. For one, you couldn't dance to save your fuckin' life. Two, somebody might see you dancing like a white man on Vicodin. Three, the high was feeling so good where you already were. Why take a chance of blowing it with massive movement?

But there was something about the way she touched your hand that made all that melt away when she led you across the grass and between the two gay dudes in tight-ass wifebeaters and a guy and girl dressed like they were trapped in summertime in '82. Tight tanktops in bright colors with different color plaid shorts. The girl's skin was so dark it seemed like a void of some kind, something you wished that you could disappear into; he looked like one of Fat Albert's homeboy's wearing a hot-ass skull cap in the dead of late spring.

The DJ blended in "Good Life" by Inner City and the crowd went crazy, and then he put something slow and dancehall behind it. You'd never heard anything like it. And Rachel made the moment perfect when she turned around and grinded that ass against you, working it to a rhythm so good that you swore to fuckin' God you were gonna bust all over yourself.

And then she kissed you right there in the middle of all those waving hands and moving hips, that sticky gloss on her lips getting all over yours. Her tongue tasted like a Nantucket Grapeade.

But then on the way home you took the train instead of a cab. And Fate brought the two of you into that same car as that nigga from Flatbush she went to nursery school with, the one who had been her man long before y'all met up at that party off of Clifton. He was jealous that you had her, that she wasn't his anymore. And he had his boys with him.

There were only three of them but you knew that was more than enough. Even if you had been Sugar Ray Leonard, three would have been more than enough to bring on the stomp-out. And you knew they were gonna come at you with the first word out of your mouth. Yet and still you had to do something, even if she said that you didn't.

You told yourself that you were gonna make those niggas remember you for life, that you were gonna mark them somehow.

To your credit, you did break the boyfriend's nose, cracked it right across the bridge and watched the blood run like a faucet. But the other two were vicious. The box cutter almost sliced your face before you kicked it to the other end of the train. You swung wild. But it was three on one. When you woke up, you had multiple slashes across both forearms and Rachel had a black eye. You would only see those dudes one more time, and that would be at Skate City.

The door opens just as the memory starts to fade. You find it strange that they took all of your personal effects—wallet, keys, and phone—but they didn't print or book you. No pictures. No charges. Strange.

Enter your pig for the evening. He's in his late thirties, with red hair cut close and a suit he bought off the rack from someplace not too respectable but just short of garbage. He has a folder in hand, which is probably full of pictures, and a pad for taking notes. He's pulling out a chair when a brother who seems a little older comes in behind him with nothing but a digital recorder and a legal pad.

They introduce themselves as Detectives A & B.

The brother takes off your cuffs. You let out a long exhale to make them think you're relieved, to give them the impression that you haven't been sitting here crafting your statement the whole time.

"Where's Tony Star?" Detective A, the redhead, asks.

You know what to say because your stepmom gave you that little booklet, *The Black Man's Handbook*, fifteen pages of things that might keep you alive and free a little longer in situations like this one. You've already committed every badge number you've seen to memory: 1412, 2382, and now these guys are 5116 and 3224.

"Am I under arrest?" you ask.

"We know you're his errand boy and that you didn't kill anybody. We want to help you."

"Am I under arrest?" you ask again, knowing that it will annoy them.

"No, but we can keep you for up to thirty-six hours right here in this room. That's a whole lot of time for somebody we're not trying to bust. We just want to know where to find Tony Star."

This would be the point—if you were some flag-waving patriot white boy—where you'd give up everything because they've told you they're not gonna bust you. For all you know, they could be trying to connect you to one of the murders or some bag of powder tucked away in the place. Try to hold out from saying anything and they'll tell you everything.

You take turns looking them in the eye, making sure they understand that you're not another dumb nigga they're gonna intimidate. You don't have a mama to cry for you, no father to be shamed if they send you away.

"We know you're a good kid," Detective B, the brother, continues. "Been on the straight-and-narrow ever since the group home, even after your parents were murdered. We know you want to help us. But we also know who you work for."

"We can protect you," Red chimes in, "move you to another borough or somewhere else."

"All we want from you are some answers, before it's too late."

You study their faces. They really need you to talk and to talk now. If they didn't, they'd be leaving the room or taking shifts or doing something a lot more devious than giving it to you straight.

"Ten people have been killed in the last seven hours and you're the only person who might be able to tell us who's responsible."

The street soldier in you says that you should hold out longer. But the longer you sit, the less chance you have of getting out of here soon. If you at least pretend to play ball you might get a ride home, maybe even a coffee from some bodega. The sun should be up by now.

"Ten? There were only six in the bar when I came in there."

A & B look like they want to jump up and do the running man. They've got you talking now. The folder comes open and you're looking dead at the ghost you created. The hole in the bartender's head seems even bigger than you remember it. They give you his name and all the background you already know.

"There was a shootout in his building. Nobody got a good look at the shooter but he worked at one of the clubs Star owns."

"What about the other three?" you ask.

"Three more of his guys had a head-on collision on Atlantic Avenue. Car flipped over. Not far from the club. Somebody had cut the brake line."

Three more of Star's men, all dead. The starting four, his first line of defense, mowed under by the monster blitz at the bar. Too many people have been killed for that little bag of money. Something bigger is going on.

"When was the last time you saw Star?" one of them asks. You decide to tell the truth, or at least enough of it to make your alibi clean.

"He sent me to get a bag from the club around 8."

"Which club?"

You tell them the name and there's a hint of recognition between them that suggests you aren't lying; it's the same club where the bartender worked. Connections are being made. Evidence is being gathered. You are the key they're looking for.

"What was in the bag?" Red asks.

"I don't know," you reply coldly. "The boss told me never to open anything I was carrying."

"Just like FedEx," the brother jokes. "What's inside is the client's business. You just get it there, right?"

You nod. They're being too friendly. You realize there's a catch. The catch is that from there they start working back in time, dropping people's names. Bink comes up. So do a few other dudes who worked for Star. The names match up with the fresh set of bodies the night has brought in. So now they know you're juiced in enough to make IDs. If you know the dead men then you know something else. This is when it starts to get annoying.

"What other pickups and deliveries have you made?" They say it in that same innocent, even tone, like it's just bonus info they're curious about because they have the time. But you know a trap when you see one. They're fishing for other places to look, for more witnesses and holes to search, to chop another leg out from under an operation that could be dead in the water even if your boss, the man missing in action, isn't lying unconscious somewhere.

"I don't remember," you say.

"Bullshit!" Red explodes. "You know and you better fucking tell us."

"I don't have a thing to tell."

"You think we let you out of a bar full of bodies because we feel like being nice? You think we can't find a piece of evidence in there that connects you to at least one of those murders? Hell, the gate in the front was halfway down. We'll at least get you for B&E."

You're surprised at how not-scared you are. You know that if they had any real cards they'd show them. You wiped your prints off the gun. Even if they find it, they can't connect the murder to you.

"Look, if I'm not under arrest, I'd like to go home," you say. "I've done my best to help you with this investigation."

You can see the temperature rising inside the brother's head. He wishes he had a phone book, a black jack, shit, maybe even an aluminum club to go to work on you like he's done to so many other street niggas. But something or someone is making you untouchable. And just as you're starting to wonder what it might be, there's a knock on the room's only door.

Red goes over to answer it and gets into a whispery conversation with a silhouette outside. The shadow's words only piss him off further and the two go back and forth, the unseen face trying to calm the Irish boy down. The brother attempts to distract you with more questions.

"How many other people does Star have working for him?"

You tell him that you don't know.

"Have you ever seen drugs or guns on the premises?"

You tell him that there are people who carry but you don't know their names, and that there's a gun behind the bar but it's registered. Give him answers but nothing to go on. Frustrate the shit out of him with your honesty that ain't so honest.

Red finishes his conversation with the shadow, comes back into the room, and whispers something to the brother that pisses him off too. Five seconds later they're uncuffing you.

"You're free to go," Red grumbles.

"Call us if you remember anything else," the brother says in equal disgust, as he puts a business card in your newly freed hand. Nice card actually. Bone-colored with a raised black font. So this is where all the tax dollars go.

You give them a nod as they all but push you out of the room, the brother in front with Red at the rear. You walk the poorly lit hallway through several sets of doors that take you back to the front desk and the sky-blue walls that look like they were painted with a toothbrush.

A lone white woman is waiting for you. She's right in front of three middle-aged Rastas cuffed together on a bench. You don't know what that's about since they aren't being processed either. But you don't care.

Red and the brother vanish into thin air. There's now an envelope in your hand filled with your personal effects. Everything is as it should be. The white woman says your name and you give her a nod.

"Want a ride?"

She is a dirty-blonde with some height to her. Five-eight or five-nine, buttery legs in dark stockings, grapefruit-sized tits, and no ass to speak of. You'd fuck if she offered it, but then again, there's very little you wouldn't fuck.

You follow her out into the beginnings of a new day. The clock on your cell says it's almost 8 a.m. The daylight is practically the color of orange juice. You haven't slept and you're starting to feel it, that vacant feeling that you're both there and not there at the same time.

You follow the clicking of her heels to a silver E-class on chrome factory rims. Something about that alone tells you that Star's fucked her. She doesn't look to the left and right, doesn't seem nervous about being this far into Flatbush, at least twenty blocks away from gentrified territory.

She unlocks your door before she gets around to her own, and you get in. You want her to start talking, to tell you who she is and how the fuck she got you out of a cop station where there was no official record of you. But your questions are answered the moment her thighs touch the upholstery of the driver's seat and her door seals.

"I'm Star's attorney."

"I figured that," you reply. "Is he still alive?"

"Why would I be here if he wasn't?" she asks, as she turns over the engine.

"Good point," you say. "Where is he?"

"I'm taking you to him now. It's a bit of a ride. You wanna grab some breakfast?"

The words bring thoughts of coffee and juice, sausage, scrambled eggs, and flapjacks. You've been running all night and your ribs are hurting like hell.

"That's cool. You got any aspirin by chance?"

She keeps her eyes on the road as she answers.

"Open the glove box."

You pop it open and there a prescription bottle half-full of pills. Thousand-milligram Ibuprofens. Everybody seems to need relief from something.

"I get migraines," she says before you ask.

You pop about five and gulp them down with your own spit, feel them start that slow crawl down your esophagus. They'll get to the pain sooner or later.

"How'd you get me outta there?"

"Star was on his way back to the bar when the cops raided it. Saw them bringing you out and called me before he went where we're headed now."

"Which is where?"

"Queens."

The Jackie Robinson is packed when she pulls onto it. Bumper-to-bumper for what seems like forever. The fatigue sets in quickly. You close your eyes and it's like falling into a well. The last thing you remember is a voice telling you that *they are on the way*. You must be losing it.

Something jerks your arm and you come alive. Drool has dried on the right corner of your mouth. The jerk is the attorney's hand.

"You still want to eat, right?"

You nod, then ask for her name.

"Jodi," she says. Her accent isn't New York, more Mid-Atlantic. Philly? DC? Virginia? "Let's go."

Queens will never be Brooklyn. It's one of those things that both boroughs understand perfectly. Thing is that people from one always thinks the other sucks dick. And it runs deep. You've never even looked at a girl from over there. The G train is the only bridge between the two worlds, a shitty rickety train that never runs the way it's supposed to. So go figure.

This diner looks like something you'd see on TV, a lot of middle-aged white broads with Long Island accents slinging coffee and flapjacks fresh off the griddle. A woman in her fifties with *Martha* on her nametag sits the two of you at a booth way in the back. What better place to put the thuggish-looking black boy and the white woman in the two-piece suit and dark stockings? You order a pot of coffee and look at the menu as if you don't already know what you're going to get. When you look up, you notice that Jodi is staring at you.

"What?" you ask, feeling fatigue pushing down on your eyelids again. Apparently the nap wasn't enough.

"You don't look like the type," she says.

"The type for what?" you ask, just as Martha returns with your coffee and a pad to put it on.

"Star," she says.

"There's a type?"

"Yeah, boys who don't know any better, that get on the wrong side of things really early, who don't have anywhere else to go."

"I'm just paying my tuition."

"There's much easier ways to do it."

Maybe it's the fact that you're tired, or nervous, or just more perceptive than usual, but it seems like she's changing into some bleeding-heart liberal in front of your eyes, like all of a sudden she gives a fuck about you and your welfare, like she wants to take your cute and cuddly ass and show you the way out of the street life. What is this, *Webster* with a broad? Your step-parents already tried that shit and look what happened to them?

"What difference does it make to you?" you ask.

She hesitates for a second, like she just let something out that she hadn't planned on. "I spring a lot of people for your employer. And you just seem different, particularly in light of all that's going on. People dead all over the place. Moves being made against your boss. You know how to stay calm, how to handle obstacles."

"I'm an orphan," you bark. "I gotta rely on me."

"Maybe, or maybe you have more fuckin' sense than most of the Star Mob, at least the ones who are left."

Her words make you think of all the bodies. There've been so many in such a long night. Some you know, others you killed, others seemed to come out of nowhere. Who would've thought that bitch could be behind all of this? Who would've thought a fuckin' dancer could almost topple this big of an empire?

The more things slow down, the more the adrenaline fades. You're starting to feel it all and it's making you scared. Jodi's words aren't helping matters either.

Martha comes back and takes your orders. You ask for French toast, sausage, and hash browns. She gets a muffin. Neither of you says anything for a few minutes after that. She looks out the window at the traffic on what the sign says is Queens Boulevard. You focus on the hugeness of the Italian waitresses tits behind the counter at the front, the way they bounce a little each time she sets a plate down. The silence keeps on until the food comes. You feel guilty that she made this stop when she didn't have to. You feel guilty for not being grateful that she's the reason you're no longer in A & B's care.

"So how long you been working for him?"

"Five years. He was my first client when I came here."

"Let me guess: Now he's your only client."

"Yeah, pretty much. How'd you know?"

"I know how he operates," you say. "He keeps his people close, real close. For better or for worse."

"I've seen both," she says with a sigh. "It's not like I wanted a 5 a.m. wakeup call. Nobody wants a 5 a.m. wakeup call."

"I hear dat," you say. "So how much do you know about this little situation?"

"Only what I need to, though I wouldn't discuss any of *that* in a place like *this*, if you understand me."

"My bad," you say. "I was just trying to make conversation."

"You can make conversation about anything, except what you would never want anyone else to hear, for either of our sakes."

"How far is where we're headed?" you ask.

"Another twenty minutes or so. Fresh Meadows isn't that far."

"Damn, I didn't think Star ever got that far out of Brooklyn."

"He goes as far as he needs to go," she grins. "I know that for sure."

She flags the check and you're out of there in another ten. Hop back in the Benz and you're on your way to meet the man, though you don't have a clue about what you're meeting up with him to do next.

5.

Fresh Meadows might as well be Pleasantville. White faces with salaries to match and a few specks of color thrown in for the sake of diversity. You actually think you saw a Dairy Queen on one block and a group of kids selling lemonade on another. Something big must be up for Star to make this kind of a retreat. He must have something out here that's too hot for The Stuy or anywhere else in Brooklyn. And you're actually a little curious to see what it is.

Jodi pulls into a subdivision of regular-looking cribs, followed by another after that. Next thing you know, you're heading up a hill to a more upscale collection of homes, like the one's you'd find in Jamaica Estates or Westchester.

"A friend of mine helped him close on this place," Jodi says. You keep glancing at her legs, the strength of her thighs. You have to respect the boss's taste.

"How long ago was that?" you ask.

"Six or seven years ago."

"Was he renting it out?"

"Oh, no, he's been living here the whole time."

Even if it makes sense, you find it hard to believe that somebody like Star would be living in a crib way out here instead of someplace close to his operations. That's the way you'd do it at least. Keep everything close. But then again, you're twenty-four and he's pushing fifty. By that age maybe everybody needs a change of scenery.

It's a big house with gray siding and shutters on the windows. The lawn is a bright green. Garage doors are closed and you spot some oversized dude sitting on the front stoop playing with his Sidekick. Just then, as if it's Fate, your own cell gets a text message. It's from Chief: *You Still Alive?*

You write him back that it's been a long night, and he asks you to come by his spot when you get free. You're telling him you will just as Jodi comes to a stop at the curb. She doesn't look like she's getting out.

"Just ring the front bell. Somebody will answer."

"What, you ain't comin' in?" you ask.

"When it comes to certain things, it's better that I *don't* see, if you understand what I'm saying."

You nod and open the passenger-side door, preparing yourself for what awaits. Then you thank her for breakfast. She tells you to remember what she said in the diner, and you give her a nod. Next thing you know, the rear of the E-class is turning the closest corner. The painkillers she gave you are holding steady, a fact you're very grateful for.

The dude with the Sidekick comes into focus as you're heading up the walk. It's Chenky, Bink's half-brother. Half-Chinese, half-black. Last you heard he was overseeing that credit card thing for Star up in New Haven. He got sent there right after you got hired, right after Bink died. Bringing him all the way down here is proof that there's a staffing shortage at the moment.

"Can I help you with something?" he asks, standing up just so that you can see him tower over you.

"Star sent for me. I'm his."

The expression on his face warms before you can finish.

"Damn, nigga, I was just fuckin' wit' you," he says, pulling you into a half-hug that brings fire back to your rib cage. "I ain't seen you in a minute."

You fight through the pain and respond, telling him that it's been two years. He asks if the pigs fucked with you and you tell him that Jodi sprung you before they really got a chance to.

"She a down-ass bitch," he smiles. "Got me outta some shit up in New Haven more than once."

You wonder how much Star's paying him to run that whole thing up in Connecticut. Maybe it's several times what you get. Maybe it's just the same. The one thing you can tell about Chenky is that he ain't exactly a fuckin' brain surgeon.

"So where the man at?"

"Downstairs in the basement. Door's open. Somebody'll tell you how to get down there."

You open the door and head inside, past the John Coltrane rug for you to wipe your feet on and the big framed poster from *Shaft* that Star got signed by Richard Roundtree at the premiere screening. You see a sectioned crème leather couch in the living room on top of a white shag carpet. A framed blow-up nude of Pam Grier hangs over it.

Through a door to the left you can see three kids over in the kitchen, all wearing black, their hair in cornrows. None of them is over sixteen. One is scrubbing the greasy range with a Brillo pad. Another is doing dishes and a third is taking groceries out of five or six shopping bags and putting them into cabinets. You've never seen any of them in your life. And they treat you as if you're not even there. So you guess it balances out.

You cut across the living room and notice the huge flat-screen plasma and home theater with a shelf as high as the ceiling filled with every crime and gangster movie you can think of: *Casino*, *Goodfellas*, *The Harder They Come*, *City of God*, *Pickup on South Street*. Tales of the streets in like seven different languages.

A man your height and just under 400 pounds squeezes through the doorway leading to the next room. He asks your name and you give it to him. It seems to be the name he's looking for.

"Boss man waitin' for you," he says in a thick Jamaican accent. He gives you a wave to follow him, his blackberry flesh jiggling with the action.

He leads you through a library office with shelves built into the walls. You peep all kinds of titles: *The Wealth of Nations*, *Invisible Man*, *The Wine of Astonishment*, *Tar Baby*, *Praisesong for the Widow*, books you've read in school and boosted from libraries. Alexis de Tocqueville, *The Fire Next Time*. You never imagined Star to be a recreational reader.

But looking at all the volumes you realize why he might trust you so much—you've remained loyal to the hood, to your people, and have still sought to better yourself. You can speak both languages and never be called into question by one or the other. Bink couldn't do that. Neither could Tiny or Dante. Maybe that's why you're still here, why you're still alive after all that's happened.

A man with salt-and-pepper hair and matching beard is standing in a corner of the library surrounded by what is easily twenty grand in computer equipment. You can tell that he's looking for something, or someone. But you keep your eye on the yardie as he leads you out of the library and down a narrow corridor he can barely fit through, to a small greenhouse just behind the garage. Upon closer inspection it's about ninety percent marijuana plants shielded from view by walls of rhododendrons. Plus there's a high fence surrounding the rear of the house. Yet another income stream for a man with too many of them.

You hear Lee Morgan playing as the yardie leads you down a few rows of plants to an open area that is empty except for the desk where Star is seated and a small boom box providing the sounds echoing through the small space. There's an Italian broad in her twenties dressing a wound on his forehead. She has that dark Sicilian complexion with long legs and a pair of tits that seem to defy gravity. Star definitely has a type, but then again, what man doesn't?

"Been a rough night, eh?" Star asks. His voice has more gravel than usual. Meadow Soprano and the yardie make themselves scarce. And now it's just you and him in the greenhouse full of trees.

"You can say that," you reply.

"Nights like these tell the world who you are."

"Whatchu mean?" you ask.

"Somebody in your position these past twelve hours, out lookin' for money they shouldn't be able to find, beaten to a fuckin' pulp. No gun, no crew, nothin' but your brain. Most people turn snitch. They leave town. They try to hide. Not you."

"I like my life," you say. "I do my job."

"So you found the money?"

"Yeah, but I stashed it when I didn't hear from you. Felt like something might be up. That's why I went to the bar."

"Good thing I took your advice about the safe, eh?"

"Yeah, but I was thinking, what if they'd tried to make *you* open it?"

"Then I woulda taken a few with me." He smiles and you force one onto your face. You're tired and the drugs are wearing off again. Your broken ribs are starting to ache again.

"It wasn't your fault," he says, his face stiffening again.

"What do you mean?"

"As you know by now, it wasn't just the girl.

Whole crew of 'em right under my nose. Plotting to take over the world."

"I took care of the bartender," you say. "That's how I got the money. They were trying to skip town with it."

The frown on his face says that you got something wrong. "I thought that too until I got a call right after you left from somebody who said they had the money. Told me to meet them at a lot out in Brownsville. Me and the boys get in the car and the brakes are cut. Car flips about three times, messed up every muthafucka in it. We crawled out right before the cops got there. Muthafuckas dislocated my shoulder. We took a car to the Starlight on Nostrand and had Trevor pick us up. We head back to the bar just in time to see this slag bitch running out, so I have Trevor grab her."

"How'd you know she had something to do with it?"

He taps a finger against his skull. "Intuition, my friend. Same thing that got *you* through your life."

Everything he says makes you more anxious. Not because of what he's saying, but because you know where it's all leading.

"What you need from me?" you ask, knowing that what he says next isn't going to matter.

"Somebody's tryin' to take my crown, break me up like de body of Christ, and have themselves a little communion. And now that I know who it is, I must show them the wrath of God."

He sounds like a villain out of an Indiana Jones flick, so corny that it's actually hard to take him seriously. But you just nod your head, pretending to listen, while you look for a way out of this thing.

"Who is it?" you ask.

Something about the question makes him smile. "I was just about you show you."

You follow him back out of the greenhouse, through the narrow hall, and into the library, where Star opens a door leading to the basement. You notice that the walls going down the stairwell aren't painted. And you can smell fresh plaster. The basement has been redone, probably recently.

Nothing can prepare you for what you see when you turn the corner. The bitch is on her knees, her mouth parted just enough to fit the little dick of the nigga with the Caesar standing in front of her, Akademiks down to his ankles. A light-skinned boy of fourteen is behind her, fuckin' her from behind without a rubber. One of her eyes is swollen shut and her arms and legs are covered in tiny slices that look like they been made with a scalpel. She's like a corpse that hasn't died, a fantasy turned sadistic fuck doll in just a few hours time.

You've never seen anything like this. You'd seen your biological old man go to town on Moms a few times. But that was mostly open fists, and only because she'd somehow managed to fuck up the game at that particular point. You've seen broads scratch each other bloody, their titties flopping in the wind for all the world to see. You've seen what a twelve-gauge does to a forty-five-year-old woman with three kids because she passed a fake Benjamin to the wrong nigga on the worst day of his life. But you've never seen anything like this. How can Star be this brutal when he himself has a little girl? And where are all these young kids coming from? What is this, the Fresh Meadows Boys Club?

There are so many thoughts it makes your head hurt. The swaying of her nipples reminds you of happier times for the two of you. You feel bad for her, even if she was going to kill you, even if this whole night is happening because of her.

"This is what the Judas bitch deserve," Star says. Another kid, this one barely twelve, appears from another room with a video camera. "We gotta get this shit on tape." Star begins to fiddle with the controls on the side of the device. He doesn't seem to know how to switch it on.

Your stomach turns. This is what you always aimed to stay away from.

Star stands next to you as if he's entertaining. The kid at her rear takes his dick out and forces it into her ass. She lets out a mere whimper, too worn and beaten to offer much more.

"What'd she tell you?" you ask Star.

"Everything I need to know. Had that an hour ago. This is just to make it last longer."

"What, you gonna kill her?"

He turns to you again and offers up that grin. "No, I was saving her for *you*."

He puts a hand on your shoulder. It couldn't be a more perfect time for the dude with the Caesar to bust in her mouth, his cum spilling down her lips like you're watching Mr. Marcus in a fuckin' porno. Her hands stop her from falling on her face as the guy pulls away and zips up. The kid is still going at it though, using her hips like handlebars, somehow knowing that this is the most thorough-bred piece of ass he'll have for a long time.

"How was it?" Star asks the Caesar as he heads to the stairs.

"Fuckin' shame she ain't gon' make it," he replies with an uncertain expression. It was probably the best head he'd ever had.

"Hurry da fuck up, bwoy!" Star yells to the other kid, who speeds up and closes his eyes. But your eyes are on her, and her one good eye is on you. She wants you to help her.

"You got a piece?" you ask, just as the kid blows his load inside of her, pulls away, and zips up. She curls into a ball and closes her eyes.

Yardie boy taps you on the shoulder and you spin around to see him holding a Glock in one hand and a pair of latex gloves in the other. You take the gloves first and then the piece.

"You gotta dump that yourself," Yardie says as he starts back up the stairs. It's just you and Star now.

You cock the pistol and test its weight in your hand. Lighter than that Beretta but just as deadly, if not more. You turn to Star.

"Can you give me a minute?"

For a moment he thinks you're kidding. But then he sees that look in your eyes, the one that says you want to do this warrior to warrior, that you want to prove to him that you've got what it takes but still give her the moment to die respectfully at the hands of her enemy.

He nods and starts up the stairs as well. You move toward her when you hear him close the door at the top.

She lets out a cough as you stand right above

her. Her eye opens and meets your own. You stare at each other for a long time. You imagine that she's thinking you sent them away so you could free her. But you're from Bed-Stuy, where fairy tales fade like pictures in sunlight. She was dead the minute they brought her down here, the minute they started doing everything they did to get her to this point, as the poster girl for crime not paying.

"Why me?" you ask her. There's a trembling in your voice you can't conceal from her.

She thinks on the question, as if the answer might save her life.

"You had the bag," she murmurs. It is now that you truly know she's a bitch, that there is no heart of gold within her once perfect body, that she was out to get you from the start, that the love you thought might have been there, or at least the loyalty, was worth only as much as you put in her garter. Nothing more.

But that doesn't make it any easier as you remove the safety. The bartender was a spur-of-the-moment thing, self-preservation. This is an execution. This is something you can't tell yourself you had no control over. But if you don't do it someone upstairs will. And the two of you will most likely end up somewhere in the trunk of the same abandoned car.

You concentrate on the pain all over your torso, the broken molar at the rear of your mouth, the taste of blood still lingering. You remember the chair landing on top of your skull, the stun gun, the bats and clubs, the shotgun. They fill you with just enough rage to aim and fire. At close range the bullet goes straight through her skull, leaving a stain the width of the carpet square on the concrete floor.

Life takes nine months to arrive and a single second to leave. It is only in this moment that you know you could've loved her. But she never would've let you.

Star, the yardie, and Caesar come downstairs a few minutes after that first shot and inspect your work. Star seems proud.

"Precise," he says, as he looks down at the corpse, then back up at you. This time there's no grin on his face. "I got one more job for you."

6.

Y ou like that shit I did with the scalpel, right?" Caesar chuckles. "Learned that shit from that Larry Fishburne movie. You know the one with that bitch from *Desperado?*"

You barely nod. The kid has been talking since you pulled out of the driveway. In less than ten minutes you know that his real name is Harold and he's from Gowanus projects. Got put on with Star through his play aunt who used to work at the bar back when he was in juvie for breaking some half-Jewish kid's arm with a bat down at the Promenade. According to Harold, the kid was short on money for some weight he was dealing, but you see him more as the stick-up kid type.

Star called Harold himself to ask if he was interested in some "extra work," and he was in his '90 Accord three minutes later. The car smells like dirt weed covered over with Lysol, which makes you want to spit. He's driving you to the LIRR, which will take you back to the neighbor-hood, where you are to perform your last task of the day. But you have to get it done without killing this asshole at the wheel who talks like Kool G Rap on helium.

The first thing that occurs to you about him is that he's never shot anybody (not to say you've bodied a slew of people either), because he's way too on your dick about what you just did.

"One shot, baby, and that bitch was outta there!" he laughs.

You're actually more frightened by his handiwork. You made your own job on her quick and far less painful than the torture he'd carried out. Causing people to suffer for pleasure is much worse to you than being the murderer you've recently become. But you try to look past all these things to how you can use him to stay alive.

"So . . . you rollin' tonight?" you ask him, mainly to see if he knows any more about the plan than you do.

"Where the fuck else I'ma be?" he asks. "Wouldn't miss goin' to war for the world." Spoken like somebody who has obviously never seen one.

"Where it supposed to be at?" you ask.

"Don't nobody know but Star. We go where he say we go."

That doesn't sound good to you. Not in the least. You're getting tired again but you don't even want to blink in this kid's presence. Don't show him any weakness, though you're nothing but it right now. For all you know, Star might've told this dude to turn your lights out. But as Queens Village station comes into view, you're pretty certain that you'll at least see Brooklyn again.

Standing on the platform, you get flashes of her face before and after: her eyes perfect and then the one swollen shut, her mascara in place and then smeared every which way beneath her eyes. You know in the end that you did her a favor. Living with what they did to her might have been too much, even for a bitch that set you up and tried to kill you twice.

There's about sixty percent chance that you'll burn in Hell for all of this. The probability will jump to eighty once this last run is over. But at least you'll have from then until Judgment Day to spend without having to look over your shoulder—as long as Star succeeds. It'll be back to deliveries as usual: quick stops at bars and clubs and cabbie outfits, picking up and dropping off, rarely knowing what you have in hand. No more guns. No more injuries. And you still have half a chance of graduating on time.

Your train pulls in and you plant yourself in a mostly empty car. If you're lucky you'll at least have a few minutes to rest your eyes and the throbbing headache above them. The sleep is bliss. Nothing but one big black space and this feeling of dissolving into it. No more pain or jittery nerves. No more racing pulse or the queasiness in your gut from a breakfast that ain't digesting so well.

You give yourself to it, savor it, only to feel it all over again when your lids pop open at Flatbush Avenue, the end of the line. You practically have to peel yourself out of the seat to get going.

Outside, the piercing daylight from above only makes your head feel worse. It's midday. You haven't slept in a full twenty-four hours. You slip into the first bodega you see and down a double dose of Red Bull, your nerves so weak you can barely crush the cans. You walk up Hanson and turn left on South Oxford. The address is 217 and you have a key to the basement entrance, courtesy of the man you still work for.

It looks like any other brownstone on the block: iron gate, little garden in front. The elderly Jewish woman on the porch across the street gives you an eye that says she ain't seen you around here before. You nod back politely, silently telling the broad to go fuck herself.

You put the key in both locks and they turn. The door comes open and you go in. Next thing you know, you're walking floors that haven't been swept in months, following the directions on the slip of paper in your hand, and only the daylight coming from the rear windows to guide you. It's the third door on your right, or at least that's what his instructions say.

But when you get to the flimsy wood door and pull it open, you find that's it's not a room, but a closet. You pull the beaded chain and white light floods the space to show you a small arsenal of more guns than you could fire in a lifetime. Your list calls for the entire rack of nines, two of the twelve-gauge shotties, a street sweeper, the AR-15, and all of the boxes of ammo that match. An empty black duffel bag hangs on a nail on the back of the door, waiting for you to fill it.

The bag is just long enough to fit in the rifles and weighs about fifty pounds once you get everything in and sling it over your shoulder. You kill the closet light, close the door, and lock the other doors behind you as well. The jet black '96 Eclipse is parked two doors down. Using the other key you've been given, you load the bag into the trunk and are about to turn the key in the ignition when your cell goes off. It's Will.

"Where you at?" he asks. With more tension in his voice than you're used to hearing.

"Fort Greene."

"You get that biz taken care of?"

"Yeah," you tell him. "Shit worked out."

"Oh, word?"

"Yeah," you reply, feeling like that was something he wasn't expecting. "What's the deal?"

"Me and Chief need to holler at you. Can you come through my spot real quick?"

You know that they know your shit is on critical, so something must really be up. And even in the middle of all this shit, they're still your boys, men who were willing to die for you when the time came. Sure, Star is expecting you at the address he gave. But you've got what he needs and there's plenty of time until the move at 10 p.m.

You start up your new ride and hit a left on DeKalb toward Flatbush and then cut over to Myrtle to get to Marcus Garvey.

7.

It's a street-cleaning day so the cars are all on the left side of the road, which means no parking close to Will's. You have to go all the way up to Decatur to find a space and then hike back down. Just a few more hours and you can find your bed. Tomorrow morning you hit the school infirmary and get looked at all over. Maybe it's mostly bruises and no more fractures. Maybe you can still be that lucky.

You see what looks like four guys moving from Will's to the corner, bodies and faces that seem familiar, but distant. They reach the intersection and turn out of sight, either heading for Fulton or for a car parked somewhere. You wonder that they're doing over at Will's so early, which makes you wonder what it is that Chief and Will might want from you.

A man old enough to be your granddad cruises past you on an old BMX, swerving from side to side without a care in the world. It would be cool to be like that when you get old, to still be so active, not just sit in the house and collect Social Security or some shit. Have a broad to wipe your mouth and shit when you die, someone to confess all your sins to. But knowing bitches in this day and age, it probably ain't gonna happen.

When you get to Will's house, you notice there's a new coat of black paint on the fence.

"Rahman did it," Chief says. He's standing in the open doorway, looking like he's been waiting for you. Rahman is Will's uncle, who helped his nephew get the grant to buy his crib. Moved down to Atlanta but he comes up about three times a year to check on things.

You force your body up the steps. Every muscle is spent. The pain is a constant hum echoing through your torso. Chief gives you a pound when you reach him and ushers you inside, locking the door behind you.

Will is in the kitchen taking a pan of steaks out of the broiler to put them on the stove. There is a bottle of Dom chilling in a Tupperware container filled with ice next to the pan on the counter. The smell of the meat makes your mouth water.

"You hungry, nigga?" Will asks as you enter.

"Fuck yeah," you say. "Especially when you setting it out like that."

"It's a celebration," Chief says, moving into the kitchen from behind you.

"What for?" you ask.

"We gon' get to that," Will says.

Chief grabs the bottle of bubbly and carries it into the dining room through a small door.

"Go on in there and sit down," Will says, and he puts the steaks and a little bit of salad from a bowl onto real plates. You're always impressed with what he can do from a wheelchair. You don't think you could be that mobile sitting down all the time. But then again, you know you'd manage if you didn't have a choice.

The table is set with linen napkins and fancy glasses. A white seven-day candle burns bright in the center as the afternoon sunlight streams in from the big window on the east wall. There are only three chairs, one for each of you.

Chief is already seated as you sit next to him. For the first time you notice the picture of Colonel Sanders, the KFC guy, on his T-shirt. You want to ask about it but you're way too tired. Besides, he gets back up to help Will with the plates before you can.

"Don't tell me one of y'all got a kid comin'," you say.

"Nah, but somebody's gonna be *goin'* tonight," Chief answers.

"What you mean?" you ask.

"You know dat pussy-ass nigga that shot us? The one we never fount?"

You nod as a chill runs through you.

"Well he fount now. Nigga name is Frank and he over in Armstrong."

"How you know it was him?"

"You know Marley from the fifth floor in our building?" Chief asks, as he takes a first bite of his steak. You're a third of the way done with yours. It's delicious. "The one your boy Bink shot in the leg over that dice-game shit?"

You nod, your mouth full of red meat.

"He just came home. Caught some assault charge and they had him on Rikers for two. So he gets to talkin' wit' some dude on his cellblock, some nigga who was out there that night and heard him bragging about it on the yard to some Queens niggas, tryna impress 'em and shit."

This is the wrong day to be hearing about this, the wrong day to look back on the blood spilled on that skating rink sidewalk. But it's here, right when you're in the middle of something else.

"But it was a whole bunch of niggas in there," you say.

"Yeah, but only two gats. Ten shots. You heard 'em. It was that muthafucka put me in this chair. And you know what he did to you."

He pours champagne into everybody's glass and offers a toast.

"To dead muthafuckas," he says. You're the last one to drink but you make sure they see you. This is, after all, an issue of loyalty, of experience, of how real boys are there for each other when it comes to what matters. They've asked you here because they want you to play a part in this execution. As to what that part will be, you're not so sure.

"You askin' if I'm in?"

Will looks at you for a long moment and then sits his glass down half-finished. He seems to have some kind of conflict about the answer.

"Nah," he says. "I don't want you near this shit—"

"Why not?" Chief interrupts. "We could always use a . . ."

"We don't know who this nigga Frank work for!" Will shoots back. "For all we know, he might be on Star's team with this nigga. He go out there with us and our boy ends up hangin' on a hook somewhere."

You see yourself hanging on a hook, like that guy with the afro in *Goodfellas*. And it ain't a pretty sight.

"Besides, you still got business, right?"

"Yeah," you say. "But it ain't nowhere near Armstrong. It's over on the—"

"Just stay above Atlantic. Do your shit and post up at your spot. It won't go that far up."

You keep quiet but your spider sense is ringing like a school bell. There's another part to this thing the two of them ain't tellin' you. Is this the first time they've kept something from you? Does it matter?

"So who in wit' you?" you ask.

Will runs down names, five or ten of them. Some of them you know. Others are from before your time or after you stopped being around so much. Either way, Will's got himself an army again. And that ain't necessarily a good thing.

You were in the backseat of that Legend he and Mike Mike jacked from that half-ass hustler in Brownsville. That Saturday was cold for April, so cold your bubblecoat didn't even make a difference it seemed like. You all went out to Queens and made the most of the whip before you ran it to the chop shop that half-Korean dude had up on Gun Hill Road. Booked some girls, took some pictures, you know, lived it like it was yours. Just before dawn, Will popped the trunk and found that brick in there, more weight than any of y'all had ever seen outside of the movies, the kind of weight that gave little boys big dreams of livin' it like Frank White. Handling the current crew in Lafayette Gardens wouldn't be that hard.

Will had the number and he knew just who to make examples of if he needed to. He was king for three months. Then y'all headed up to Skate City for that birthday party and it all changed.

"You sure this is what you wanna do?" you ask them.

"This nigga almost killed you," Will replies. "You sayin' you want his ass walkin' and talkin'? I know I don't. And I know Chief don't, college boy. Don't forget where you was before Prince Charming came."

He gives you that look that says you should know better than to say something back, that hard cold stare that would make almost anybody flinch. But not you. Not tonight. He was right. You've crossed over now and there's no turning back, even if he doesn't have a clue.

"I just don't want y'all to . . ." You intentionally let your voice trail off, playing up the fact that you don't want your boys to get bodied over this. You want him to remember when they had the both of you in that same ICU for a week, when you talked about God and how none of this shit was worth it.

Difference was that you walked out of there and he never would again. You went to school and he had to learn how to live without legs. Least his dick still worked, but he's always had a little envy about that shit, something you more than understand. Now somebody's gotten in his ear again, pulling all that hate up from the darkness, and he wants the head that took his legs away. And he's got more than enough niggas down for the cause. He doesn't need you and you don't need this. Get that bag to Star and get yo' ass home. The chips will have fallen by tomorrow morning.

"Don't worry, nigga. Who the fuck you think you talkin' to?" He smiles and you and Chief do the same.

The rest of steak and champagne is nothing but lovely. Chief tells you about a Senegalese girl he's in love with who lives up on Prospect. Will says he wishes his girl would turn up pregnant so he'd have a reason to get married. All the things on your mind fade to the background as you enjoy a few minutes with your boys, minutes together that may or may not be your last.

Coming out of the house, you feel the buzz in your limbs on top of the fatigue. The walk back to your car feels longer than it should. As you turn the car over, you think about your birth father, about how he lived like this damn near every day. You remember the circles under his eyes from not sleeping, the way he floated in and out of your young life like a ghost, offering money and words of wisdom you would barely remember and never understand—until now.

"World is like a washing machine, boy," he would say sometimes, when he volunteered to put you to bed. "People packed into a tight, hot space where they drown and then dry out over and over again. You come here to get clean but you still end up dirty some kinda way."

8.

There's a parking space for you at the corner of Patchen and Jefferson. A group of old men are gathered at the bodega on the corner, wasting the day away because there's nothing else to do. You give them a respectful nod as you open the trunk and grab the bag of artillery. It seems heavier now.

You trudge down the block about six brownstones, walk up the stoop, and ring the bell and wait. You notice four girls playing double-dutch a few houses up. You're about to ring the bell again when Tyren comes barreling down the stairs to the door. He's about six-six and 300 pounds, Jamaican to the core, and a good-ass player at dominoes. But as the bracelet on his wrist reminds you, he's on house arrest while he waits for his manslaughter trial. Hit some nigga in the face at a club and killed him, that nose-against-the-brain thing.

"You got it?"

You nod and hand him the bag.

"Sorry it took me a sec, got a little company upstairs." His wifebeater is stained with sweat, so you know what he's probably been doing. "Star say for you to go home. He'll call if he need you."

You could jump for joy at those words. But you play it cool. You give Tyren a pound and he pulls you into a massive hug.

"Good to see you," he says. "It's been awhile."

"Same here," you tell him. "We miss you around the bar."

"What a fucked up night," he frowns. "Wilfred was my man." You nod, thinking about him and the others, about how no matter what they had done, these were people you worked with, who you saw out in the street, and now they're gone, just like the bartender, just like that bitch. It's as if somebody picked apart your whole world piece by piece in one night. Any blood Star plans to spill won't change that. In truth, it will only make things worse.

"It'll get handled," you say, reaching up to put a hand on his shoulder. "But I'm out, man."

He turns around without another word and heads his way as you head yours. The sun is just above the horizon and night is on the way. Adrenaline has gotten you through the day, and now it's time to come home.

* * *

You wanted a ground-floor apartment but you ended up with a joint on the fourth floor. You can feel the burn in your thighs when you get to the top. Apartment 4R never looked so good.

On the other side of the door you head straight for the bathroom, plug the tub, and start running the water. You add Epsom salt and turn toward the mirror and begin to undress. Beneath the shirt and the vest there are plenty of black bruises, but when you touch the right side of your ribs they don't seem further damaged than earlier. You remove the tape from the left side, knowing some doctor is gonna see you soon, and even it isn't so bad. When the tub is halfway full with hot water, you switch the faucet to warm and get a beer from the fridge. No better way to cool down from all of this, no better way to put it all behind you until morning.

The water is like a million white-hot needles when you first climb in, stabbing at every sore spot. But after a few minutes it's more like a warm hug. You lean your head against the shower wall so you won't slide under if you fall asleep. You turn on the little radio in there, the one that Rachel got you. You turn it to the old-school station. Marvin Gaye is singing, a song you think you've heard before but you can't remember the name. If only you had an L to go with all of this.

You close your eyes and let the water do the work.

You dry off, shave, and check the damage. Ribs feel a little better. Tooth is still broken. Lip's not as swollen but the bruises on your face have darkened. What happened to that sweet little kid that did his homework? Life, you guess.

You kill the radio and all the lights, lock the door, sit your cell on the nightstand, and lie down. It feels like you are resting on a cloud. And once you close your eyes, that's all she wrote.

S o what school you go to?" you ask her. Two minutes earlier you were watching her phat ass switch from side to side as she did laps around the rink, jeans hugging hips round as a planet.

"Prospect," she says, nibbling on the gum between her teeth. She's got three gold bracelets on her right wrist and a Trini accent. She tells you her name is Dara.

"I don't know anybody that go over there," you say. You don't really care about school but this is the way these conversations go. You talk about school and what neighborhood you're from. Maybe you know somebody in common. Maybe she lives close. Anything to keep the conversation going. Because the longer it does, the better chance you have of getting the digits.

"So who you come here with?"

You tell her your boys Will and Chief and Chief's cousin Remi. She nods along, watching you peek down at the thick line of cleavage stuffed into her top.

"Who you up here with?"

"My sister and my cousins," she says, pointing to a group of girls over by the lockers snarling at you. Girls seem to hate seeing their friends get any play.

"How long y'all been up here?" you ask. She says it's been a couple hours, that they're about to turn in their skates and go home.

You tell her you want her to stay awhile. She says her father wants her home by 10 and it's getting close to 9:30. You ask her for her number and she says she can't give it out but she has a pager. You provide the pen and paper and she writes it down. She smells like sandalwood oil and you get the impression her eyes ain't really hazel, but those melons of hers will make up for everything else once you get that bra unclasped, get her up to your room, and introduce her to that "special friend" of yours.

She tells you to page her later, after her daddy goes to sleep, and then she can call you on the house phone. She likes that better than having to go out in the street and use a pay phone. You tell her it was nice to meet and she gives you a hug. Her lips brush against your neck a little bit and your soldier comes to attention. You watch her walk back to her friends and see that the ass ain't bad either.

Oh how you'd love to caress that thing with her on your lap, straddling you, some trees and that *Friday* bootleg on. Shit would be sweet. But that's for later. Right now you gotta find your crew. And on a Saturday night at Skate City, that shit ain't gonna be an easy feat.

Heads are fuckin' everywhere: lining the walls, moving back and forth in big crews, covering the sidewalks out front. Will and his little cartel went out front an hour ago to do some business and they still ain't back yet. Chief went with him, or maybe he went home. He did say he had to go to church in the morning.

As you start toward the exit, you bump into your boy Nyere from the third grade. He's a big muthafucka now. Says he got his GED and went to college a year early. He wants to be a lawyer. You tell him good luck and all that, but he keeps running his mouth, getting all up in your mix about Jesus and how he can save your life. You should come to his church in the morning, it'll help you see all the truth in the world. You give him a Chris Calloway juke and squeeze through a hole in the crowd, letting it close in front of him so he can't follow.

There's a girl right outside the front door slobbing down her boyfriend. His hands are palming one of the biggest asses you've see in a while: all firm, so phat that it pushes the back of her tennis skirt high enough for you to almost see her panties. You are an envious boy.

Will, Chief, Larry, Steve, Mike Mike, and Popcorn are right in the middle of it, talking to two other dudes who look like they got a problem. You move in to investigate.

"Hey, man, I just got sent to give you the message," one of them says. His shirt has a leopard print on it and he's wearing patent leather shoes with metal tips—like that shit didn't stop bein' cool in '89. Must be Jamaican, you think.

"You tell that muthafucka he need to ease up on makin' threats," Will says, loud enough for everyone to hear him. "Let him know I'ma get mine!"

The other kid in the hoodie speaks up. "You sure that's what you wanna do?"

You're right up on them now, coming to the rear of all the niggas from the Gardens ready to protect one of their own. You move to the edge of the semicircle next to Mike Mike.

"I think you hear us," Will says, putting a hand on his nuts as if all his power rests there. Even though he's shorter than you he's standing tall, ready for anything.

"So be it," Leopard Man says.

You see the dude in the hoodie reaching behind himself and you clock him across the jaw. Mike Mike kicks the dude's legs out from under him and the two of you start to stomp, one foot after the other. The blood comes quickly as you take turns. You make it so he can't even get to that heat in the small of his back.

You can hear the others taking on Leopard Man. Will is making an example, showing these dudes what happens when you cross the new players in the game. This is how it works. There's no way around it. You play your part because you know any man here would do the same for you, and they have: when those niggas from Marcy tried to rush you outside the Mobb Deep show, when them niggas checked you in for your leather on the C train and then you caught that dumb nigga wearing the coat down on Fulton Street. Last time you saw him he still had a limp.

This is your moment to prove just how down you are, how the hood still matters even if you got moved away by a few blocks. Hoodie gets a finger on the gun and you kick it away, breaking half his hand in the process. He screams. This is a shining moment, something you think you'll look on with pride for the rest of your life.

You turn around and see Will literally jumping on top of Leopard Man. The voice underneath him sounds like a six-year-old girl's. You start laughing, then so does everybody else. The shit is so funny—until you feel something approaching.

It's a dark blue Villager with tinted windows, so close to the curb it might as well be on it. The arm that holds the pistol is fully extended. The side door opens and there's another gun as well.

You try to cut right but you're not fast enough. You feel the one that grazes your ear but not the one that pierces your lung or the one that squeezes between vital parts to go in and out of your stomach. You don't see Will get hit. You don't see the pregnant girl lose an eye or Mike Mike and Popcorn take those slugs straight to the head, lights-out style. You just remember thinking—no matter how silly it is—that your book report is due next Wednesday.

9.

You think you're dreaming when Biggie's "Warning" enters the silence out of nowhere. Then you realize that it's your cellphone. Your eyes open. The clock on the nightstand says it's 11:56. For a moment you imagine it's just another day, then it all floods back. You grab the phone and flip it open. You don't recognize the voice over the gunfire in the background.

"They comin' for you, nigga! Get the fuck outta there!"

You want to ask questions, but just then you hear the rumbling of footsteps coming up the stairs. You grab the folding chair in the living room and prop it up against the door right as somebody rams it from the other side. You've got five seconds before they start shooting. You grab your pants, shirt, and shoes and head out the fire escape.

You hear your front door come down when you are two stories below on the fire escape. They can see you from your window by the time you're on the ground. Knowing that they have a clear shot if you go for the fence, you turn into the narrow passageway where Mr. Simpson, the super, keeps the garbage cans, and you head for the door that'll bring you out to the lobby. But the niggas in the jeep in front of the building see you before you realize this move was an even worse idea.

The Eclipse is parked right on the corner and you have the keys. But if they're holding, the thirty seconds you need to turn a car over will be a countdown to death. So you take off on foot down Pacific. The cars, of course, follow.

You push it to high speed as you cross Classon and enter a bodega you know has a rear entrance with a ladder to the roof at the back. Some old-school shit some kid from school showed you one time.

You storm into the joint and the four Arabs on deck all look like they're about to reach for something.

"Behind me!" you scream, hoping they'll pull out the artillery on the other niggas instead of you, except you don't hear them come in as you're clearing the rear entrance.

Your hands are raw with rust and flaking paint when you get to the top. The roof is solid. The rest of the ones on this block seem to be the same. But they've got three cars, so you're sure they're posting themselves around the block, just waiting for you to come down so they can use you for target practice.

You need to look over the edge but you're afraid to. Five minutes ago you were off in the darkness of deep sleep. Now you're on a fuckin' rooftop with no heat and no way out. Then you hear a sound that is nothing less than Savior: 5-O.

Sirens are now flooding the scene. You slither over to the roof's edge and look down. Cop cars are everywhere, but there are no jeeps in sight. Then you feel the cold steel against the back of your neck.

"Mr. Star's looking for you," the voice says. You roll over on your back to see the face that came out of Will's crib just a few hours ago: Marley, the one who told Will about Frank being the shooter at Skate City. It all comes together in your head in an instant. You don't like the picture but it's plain and clear. You know why everything has gone down tonight and why Will and Chief are about to be dead niggas if you don't do something—namely, shake the fool with the Glock standing over you.

He's alone and about your height. Head to head it might be easy to get the gun from him, but ain't no James Bond shit gonna work for you when you're at the edge of the roof and he's got a pistol two feet from your face.

"How long you been down wit' the team?" you ask.

He looks to the left and right to make sure he's by himself, which he is. "Since yesterday. Had a nigga inside who told me to come and see him." Unless you cut off his head, Star will always grow new arms.

"So what, you supposed to put one in my head?"

"Nah, man," he grins. "He just wants you to see something."

"What about the cops down there?"

He grins to show you that he's missing a top front tooth and two on the bottom. "They're gonna give us a ride."

As you start down the ladder, you see two uniforms at the bottom waiting for you. You wonder how much it costs Star to keep pigs in his pocket. They cuff you and Marley like you are perpetrators and put you in the back of a cruiser.

The two of them go back and forth about the Utah/Chicago series in '98, about how much of a hater Malone was in the interview after Jordan hit that last jumper. This shit is just business as usual. They drive you about six blocks to the Star

Lounge, uncuff you, and give Marley his pistol back, which he keeps close as he leads you inside.

This spot is like Part 2 of the old bar, the former place of employ for that team of thieves that started this whole thing. The scene is mostly Caribbean men between thirty and sixty drinking Mount Gay and listening to rockers on the house system.

All eyes are on you as Marley pushes you toward the back and into the manager's office, which is packed to capacity with soldiers. Caesar and the kids from the Fresh Meadows house are only a fraction of them. And they're all loading and cocking the weapons you delivered.

Star is at the desk putting shells into a sawed-off shottie. He grins when he sees you. The whole room goes hush the moment he speaks.

"You ready?"

The boys all turn to you, their older brother, to see if you'll accept the challenge.

"It was never because of my father, was it?" you ask. "It was because of Skate City."

"Frank went way over de line with what I told him to do. Nigga was an idiot. When I heard about you and figured out who you were, I felt like I owed Melvin's boy something—a job, an opportunity. You were out of de neighborhood,

goin' to school. Figured you had de sense to leave
a hothead like Will where he be. And for de most
part, you did . . . But I know de bwoy wasn't
finish. He just restin' for a while. I knew he'd
come at me again, and when you got hit for the
drop I could smell him all over it."

"There ain't no Frank, right?"

"Oh, dere's a Frank, but he ain't in the projects
at Armstrong. He's . . . well . . . he's all over de
place."

"So what's at Armstrong?"

"*We're* gonna be—that includes you," he says.
"In a room like this you got two choices, my
friend. Pop in a clip or get one popped into you."

The young guns all snarl at you, as if you're
rocking the boat, fuckin' up their program, even if
they have no real idea of what the program is, of
the road this will all lead them down. It doesn't
register to them that all the men who've died in
the last day started out in a room like this, that
they are taking the place of some soldier who fell
for less than nothing.

He'll make you kill Chief and Will yourself,
while he watches. The question he doesn't have to
ask is how much your life is worth. How loyal are
you to him?

There's a .45 sitting on the desk that no one
has taken for their own. You squeeze through a

few guys and grab it. You check the clip and it's filled to the tip.

"When do we do it?" you ask.

Someone pats you on the back. Caesar gives you a pound. Star comes over and offers you a gentleman's handshake.

"Welcome to my family for real, my friend, de only one you'll ever need."

10.

The ride down Bedford to Lexington is the longest ten minutes of your life. One jeep and two vans. One of Marley's boys must be with Will, steering him toward where they need to be. Star is right next to you, so a cell call is out of the question. And yelling "look out" once you're already on them won't do much. What you have to hope is that either Will called the shit off or that he's smart enough to have a plan. You also have to hope that you'll still be alive in the morning, for the second night in a row.

Ls are traveling around the car in shifts but you wave them away when it's your turn. Even Star takes a few pulls.

"This is good weed," he says to you, like a father speaking to a newly acquired son.

"I like my head clear when I go to war," you say.

"I know your choice wasn't easy," he says wholeheartedly. "But *you* always gotta worry about *you*."

You nod, knowing that he's right. But either way you're gonna be fucked. You crossed the line with the bartender and you can't go back, at least not while Star's still alive.

You're taking deep breaths by the time you reach Gates, trying to center yourself like they said to do in that meditation class you took once. You think about shooting Star in the head and then taking one for the team. But then you remember that it looks like Will was the one who got these muthafuckas to rob you in the first place, who put you in danger at the start of this thing. He ain't nobody to die for either. He ain't your friend. You are all alone now. All you can do is make the best moves for you.

"I can't wait to see the look on these niggas faces," Caesar says from the shotgun seat. "I can't fuckin' wait to get some notches on my belt." This boy needs Jesus.

You tighten your grip as the projects come into view, desperate to breathe the fresh air outside. All you can smell is the funk of too many men everywhere. You have to get out of there. But when the dark blue Villager brakes in the middle of the intersection, and when the side door comes open, you're not sure if you'll get the chance.

Seeing the moment before they do is what probably saves your life, as the gunner lets loose with something automatic and long-range. It hits the tires and the driver and Caesar, and in seconds the jeep is dead in the water. That's when the bullets come from behind, piercing Star and Marley, who are right next to you. You get the door open fast enough to tumble out onto the asphalt, bullets landing everywhere around you. Your guns slides out of reach.

Others try to get out of the ride behind you, but they get shredded like wheat before they hit the ground. Something tells you to stay down, play dead, wait for them to check you. Maybe it's someone you know. Then you can tell your side of the story. And it's right then that the gunfire stops. All of it. You look up just in time to see the van pull away, just in time to see shadowy figures vanishing from the rooftops above. You won't have the chance to plead your case. There's no time to confront your homeboys' betrayal or hear their side of the story.

The sirens come out of nowhere.

You hurt all over from the fall, but you don't seem to be hit. You stand up and take enough of a damage survey to know that everybody else is dead. You kick the pistol with your prints on it into the gutter and start running, faster than you did before, down streets, through alleys. You zigzag all the way to Fulton Street, where you hop the A to Queens to the airport, to your ride.

It's just after midnight when you pull your truck out of the lot and pay what you owe. The whole time you try to think of any evidence that might connect you to what's gone down. Sure there might be partial prints on the guns, but in truth, none of them even got used. All the soldiers and their general got taken out before the battle even began.

You wiped one gun and tossed the other. The bitch and the bartender are dead, and unless you have it all wrong, Will may very well now run Brooklyn from a wheelchair. The whole time you were nothing but a pawn, being played by both sides because you were in the wrong place at the wrong time when the whole thing started.

Will put that crew of thieves together to hit you, knowing that it would draw Star's attention away from everything else. Set up a meet and then cut the brake lines on his car. The plan must have been to take out his boys in groups. Tell the thieves that their prize is in the office. Whatever it is, they'd believe in it enough to do all the dirty work. And by the time they were done, Star should've been dead anyway.

But the big boss lived through the car crash and the thieves got taken out. Star's ready to go to war—lead Will and his crew to some building in the projects and wipe them off the face of the earth.

But somebody tells Will the real deal. Maybe Marley was playing both sides from the middle. Maybe Chief had a wire on Star. Hell, maybe he had a wire on you. If he could break into the phone company, hacking into your cell company's GPS isn't that unbelievable.

But there are still loose ends. Who called you and told you to get out of the apartment when Star was only trying to pick you up? Was it Chief? Was it Will? Was it Detectives A & B? Everything isn't wrapping itself up into a nice little bow. Instead there's nothing but an ever-increasing body count.

At first it seems like a good thing that you're the last man standing, that you lived to tell the tale. But Will might want to sweep his homeboy into a grave if he thinks you'll snitch on him. After all, you're the only one who can corroborate the whole plan, who can connect all the murders and machinations that have made up the last twenty-four hours.

Why wouldn't he kill you now, knowing that you probably suspect that he put the bitch and her crew onto that score in the first place. Truth is, you'll never know now without the risk of getting killed trying to find out.

It's pushing 2 a.m. when you get back to Brooklyn. You stay on the backstreets even though those two cops couldn't have gotten a warrant for you this fast. You zigzag and sometimes go in loops just to be safe. The weight of it all hits you when you notice the tiny specks of blood all over your gear. You'll need to change soon. But first things first.

The old house is just as you left it those hours before, and money's still there. You sling it over your shoulder and get back in the ride. You left it running the whole time. You don't want to go back to your crib though. Cops might be all over it, and even if they're not, a kicked-in door might have them there in the morning.

If you were a little dumber, you'd tell yourself you could stay in town, move out to Queens or the Bronx and put all this shit behind you. But if you stay you'll be constantly looking over your shoulder until you leave. You'll be strolling that campus quad always waiting to take one in the chest from some sniper on the roof.

You've got enough dough to make some smart moves somewhere else. You need to do that.

You're on your way to the Holland Tunnel when you suddenly loop back around. There's one last person you need to see.

You idle in front of Rachel's house imagining

what it would be like if you banged on the door and told her this whole story. What if she said she still loved you? What if she was willing to go with you where you were headed, make it like the old days and all? But maybe it's a sign from God that a Benz pulls up in front of her building just as you're about to go see.

The car drops off a woman with Rachel's complexion and a baby in her belly and about forty pounds on top of what you remember. She glances over at you, and when your eyes lock she sees nothing but a stranger. Another dream dies just as quickly as you birthed it.

You're just passing the Rahway exit on the New Jersey Turnpike when you get to thinking. Your life, as Will of all people predicted, is now over. And maybe that's a good thing. No family. No ties. Just a name and a Social Security number, just twenty-four years under your belt and no health problems to speak of once these new wounds heal. Maybe you'll make both sets of parents proud. Make they'll all spin in their graves. Either way, it's up to you and only you.

The choice is yours, so choose.

Also from **AKASHIC BOOKS**

BROOKLYN NOIR edited by Tim McLoughlin
350 pages, trade paperback, $15.95
*Winner of Shamus, Anthony, and Robert L. Fish Memorial
awards; finalist for an Edgar Award and a Pushcart Prize

*Brand new stories by: Pete Hamill, Kenji Jasper,
Arthur Nersesian, Ken Bruen, Sidney Offit, Maggie
Estep, Nelson George, and others.*

"An excellent collection of Brooklyn stories that I
urge everyone to read."
—Marty Markowitz, Brooklyn Borough President

D.C. NOIR edited by George Pelecanos
282 pages, trade paperback, $14.95

*Brand new stories by: George Pelecanos, Laura
Lippman, Kenji Jasper, Norman Kelley, and others.*

"[D.C. Noir] offers a startling glimpse into the
cityscape's darkest corners . . . [with] solid writing,
palpable tension and surprise endings."
—*Washington Post Book World*

BECOMING ABIGAIL by Chris Abani
128 pages, trade paperback, $11.95
*A selection of the *Essence Magazine* Book Club and the
Black Expressions Book Club; a *New York Times* Editor's
Choice

"Compelling and gorgeously written, this is a
coming-of-age novella like no other. Chris Abani
explores the depths of loss and exploitation with
what can only be described as a knowing
tenderness. An extraordinary, necessary book."
—Cristina Garcia, author of *Dreaming in Cuban*

SOUTHLAND by Nina Revoyr
348 pages, trade paperback, $15.95
*A *Los Angeles Times* best-seller

"What makes a book like *Southland* resonate is that it merges elements of literature and social history with the propulsive drive of a mystery, while evoking Southern California as a character, a key player in the tale."
—*Los Angeles Times*

A PHAT DEATH by Norman Kelley
260 pages, trade paperback, $14.95
*A Nina Halligan Mystery

"Nina Halligan takes on the recording industry and black music in Norman Kelley's third outrageous caper to feature the bad girl PI . . . Once again outspoken social criticism fires the nonstop action."
—*Publishers Weekly*

ADIOS MUCHACHOS by Daniel Chavarría
245 pages, trade paperback, $13.95
*Winner of a 2001 Edgar Award

"Daniel Chavarría has long been recognized as one of Latin America's finest writers. Now he again proves why . . ."
—William Heffernan